Field of Innocence
The Euphoria Series

By Lainy Lane

Published by

Redeeming Tree Publishing

Hiram, GA 30141

Copyright © 2013 Lainy Lane

All rights reserved.

ISBN: 1484032233
ISBN-13: 978-1484032237

Dedication

For my husband,

For always believing in me, no matter how crazy the dream. For always encouraging me. For putting up with my crazy obsessions of fantasy worlds, even though you don't understand them. For knowing me better than I know myself. For never letting me forget my talents, even though I bury them. For knowing I could do this and that I needed to do this. For never leaving my side, no matter how hard I made it to stand next to me. I love you with all that I have.

For my God,

For never giving up on me, even when I tried to give up on you. For finding me even in the darkest of circumstances and leading me back home. For giving me comfort in times when it shouldn't be possible. For allowing me to be a daughter of the one true King. You gave me the talent to write, I vow to use it to bring you glory and I pray that I please you in all I do.

Contents

	Prologue – Destiny	11
1	Drowning	15
2	Trust	29
3	Ruined	39
4	No Apology	59
5	Secrets	69
6	Purpose	91
7	Control	111
8	Questions	127
9	Power & Temptation	145
10	Field of Innocence	157

11	Gifted	173
12	Captive	185
13	What is Love?	199
14	Possibilities	229
15	Lies	245
16	Only Tempts	267
17	Right & Wrong	277
18	Masquerade	291
19	Mystery	311
20	True Colors	325
21	Vision	343
22	Return	355
23	Save You	367
	Epilogue – Ghost of You	381

Acknowledgements

This book is sold subject to the condition that it will not be lent, re-sold, duplicated, or circulated in any way without the previous written consent of the publisher in any form of binding or cover other than the original form it is published in and without the same conditions being imposed on the subsequent purchaser.

Text Copyright 2013 Lainy Lane
All Rights Reserved

Model: Maria Amanda Schaub
http://mariaamanda.deviantart.com/
Photographer: Helle Gry Schaub

This is a work of fiction. All characters and events portrayed are fictitious and products of the author's creation. Any resemblance to actual events or persons, living or deceased, are coincidental.

LAINY LANE

Luke 11:35-36

See to it, then, that the light within you is not darkness. Therefore, if your whole body is full of light, and no part of it dark, it will be just as full of light as when a lamp shines its light on you.

LAINY LANE

Prologue
Destiny

Love, hope, and passion...

These are the true emotions that keep us going daily. The fuel to our fires. A reason to wake up every morning, put our feet on the ground, and go. No matter how hard life gets, these emotions still lay in wait to bring the sunshine back through, eventually. That's why we keep going, why we keep waiting to see what's coming up just around this turn. The decision that we have to make is what we allow our love, hope, and passion to lie in.

Destiny. Some people buy into it, others don't. Some will base their entire lives around what destiny will do for them. Does destiny make us who we are? Do we have any control over what our lives become or is everything predestined? Are we simply followers of the uncontrollable? Is there some entity that sits in the heavens with our entire futures mapped out already that laughs at us as we desperately try to mold ourselves into something we can never truly become?

Some say destiny is what keeps us alive. It's what turns our lives into the wonderment that it's meant to be. They believe that, driven by passion, destiny leads us into the happiness and fulfillment we were made for.

Others think that destiny can be cruel. They are the ones that would rather stay on a path other than the one they find themselves walking down. Regardless of what you believe, eventually you learn that no matter how hard you try to run, what you're meant to be will always find you. You can't hide from your true self, even in times when it's all you want to do.

Life is fragile, and not only in the mortal sense. It's like a big glass ball waiting above your head; sometimes one simple event can send the glass crashing down around you into a million tiny pieces. All you can do when this happens is helplessly stand by and watch as the fragments of your world shatter, fall, and settle around you. At this point, you are faced with two choices: you can try and piece the shards back together or you can start all over and try to build a new life...hopefully a better one.

Somewhere in-between those two options is where you find the person you're actually meant to be. You find the person who's strong enough to take the on the world and face what you're intended for, no matter how impossible that may seem.

LAINY LANE

Chapter 1
Drowning

The music pulses through her blood as the noise beats out of the speakers. She can feel her heart pulse in tune with it. Calandra's body tenses with its every beat. Everything about music makes her feel alive; she needs music to feed her soul. Not that anyone in her family has ever been into music, so where she inherited the love of it is something she's never understood. But as far back as she can remember, music has always been her muse.

On this particular morning, the tune lifts her more than normal since she's already in a good mood. Chase, Calandra's uptight and completely over bearing dad, is leaving in a few days to go on a four-month business project that will take him out of the country. It wasn't easy to convince him that at 17 years old, she is perfectly capable of staying home alone while he's gone. But by some miracle he had finally folded and given into her requests. Today is the last day of her junior year in high school, and to top it all off she's on her way to pick up her boyfriend, Tristan, for school.

Given all of the circumstances, even despite being out before the sun is up, which in Calandra's opinion is a sign that it's simply too early to be awake, she still finds herself in a good mood. Her iPod switches songs and she immediately smiles when she hears Paramore. Her fingers subconsciously strum on the steering wheel as her every thought and emotion gets caught up into the song. Just as it happens all too often, the lyrics carry her off to another world, a world all her own.

A black and seemingly endless in depth body of water lies in front of her. She stands, barefoot, on the grainy rocks that surround the murky water. Everything is completely dark. Shadows seem to loom all around her, waiting to engulf her at any moment. Something floats in the water and catches her eye. She walks over to examine it further. Calandra leans over the edge of the water, careful to steady herself as she does so, and peers into the water. She sees a reflection, but it's not hers.

Dark blonde, almost brown, curly hair falls far below the woman's shoulders. The aqua green eyes seem ever so inviting. Her skin is soft and pale, too pale and her expression is weary.

"Mom?" Calandra whispers softly.

Calandra has only ever seen pictures of her Mother, and she certainly hadn't been that pale in any of the pictures. Hollyn passed away while giving birth to Calandra. Despite never meeting her Mother, Calandra has always felt as if she knew her. Hollyn has been appearing in Calandra's dreams and thoughts ever since she could remember.

The reflection in the water reaches its arm out towards Calandra. Calandra slowly starts to reach toward her mothers arm and fully expects to touch cold water. No water saturates her skin, instead she feels a hand- her mother's hand. It wraps around hers and grips around her wrist far too tightly before it pulls Calandra into the water.

Calandra's chest freezes and she can't breathe when she first hits the water. Ice forms inside her chest, thick and heavy. Her lungs fill with water and she feels herself start to weigh down and drop quickly. The water is cold and viscous and Calandra can't see through it no matter how hard she tries. She thrashes her arms around frantically but feels nothing other than the freezing cold waters as they rush around her and suck her down. Her heart races. She focuses all of her strength, every fiber of her being, towards the efforts to swim back to the surface. But no matter how hard she fights against the currents, she simply isn't getting anywhere. She feels the hand of her mother wrap around her once more and a sense of security falls over her. She knows she has help now.

But the arm pulls her the wrong way and the water gets darker and colder. She tries to pull away but there's no use. Calandra watches helplessly as her mother pulls her all the way to the bottom of the water. Her leg sinks down into the ground and she realizes this is where her life will end. Just as she runs out of breath and is left with no choice but to breathe in a mouthful of the icy water, she jolts back to reality.

She gasps deeply as she tries to catch her breath again. Her heart feels like it is going to beat out of her chest. Swim in Silence ends on her iPod and immediately switches to an upbeat tune. Calandra looks around frantically. She blinks rapidly in hopes of making the vision of her mother go away, but it proves to be pointless. A horn honks behind her and she realizes she is sitting in the middle of the road and holding up traffic. She hits the gas pedal harder than she needs to and the car jolts alive and the tires screech as she takes back off.

"Breathe Cali." She reminds herself as she turns up the music to help her calm down.

Her heart begins to slow back to an almost normal rate and the cold, which she somehow still feels in her chest despite now being checked back into reality, starts to subside. She breathes in slowly and blows the breath back out of her mouth. She thinks carefully about every move she makes in hopes it will keep her thoughts away from anything else. Warmth slowly creeps back into her as the words of the song that plays through the speakers carries her back into the beat. Once again, her muse takes everything else away and makes the world seem as right as it had been before the daydream.

Daydream isn't quite the word Calandra would choose to describe her experiences, but it's the word her dad always uses. These experiences have plagued her ever since she can remember.

They don't feel like make-believe, but that is of course what her dad has always insisted they are. She feels things in them, she can smell things in them, a few times she's even tasted things. She doesn't feel like she just gets lost in her thoughts, it all feels real. Sometimes they are about her mother. Sometimes they are about a woman who she assumes to be her great grandmother. Although all she knows about Echo is what little her father, who obviously hated her, had told her several years ago after she described the woman from her experience to him.

"She was a crazy woman Cal," her dad had scoffed, "but she did love her family. That's really all I choose to say about her." Then after clearing his throat and rolling his eyes he had walked away. Calandra hadn't dared to bring it up again.

She pulls into Tristan's driveway and shuts off the car to wait for him. She picks up her cell phone to send him a text and let him know she's waiting. Before she can hit the send button, her passenger door opens. Calandra jumps as Tristan's head pokes in and he laughs at her.

Tristan has olive skin and dark hair long enough in the front to cover part of his eyes if he doesn't sweep it away. His hair spans across his ears and hangs almost to his shoulders in the back. He is on the small side but much stronger than he looks. He is far from your average high school football quarterback. He wears skinny jeans, Converse shoes, and usually nothing but band T-shirts. Most days he puts color on the tips of his bangs; today the color of choice is blue.

Calandra hates that he lets his hair cover his eyes so much. His eyes are what had first attracted her to him. She finds that no matter how many times she sees him, his eyes will still take her breath away every time they peer through his hair at her. They are the most beautiful shade of baby blue; crystal clear, bright and invigorating. Calandra always seems to get lost in them, somehow she knows if she stares long enough she'll get a glimpse straight into his soul.

"Good morning beautiful." He smiles as he gets into the car and gives her a soft kiss on the cheek.

Calandra's cheeks turn red and she feels the heat rise into them. Somehow even after 7 months together he still has the ability to make her blush and take her breath away.

"Good morning." She replies as she puts the car back into gear and pulls out of the driveway. She turns the music down once they are on the road again. Calandra watches the trees and road lines pass by them. She tries to focus on anything she can to keep from reliving the daydream again. Tristan slowly runs his hand through her hair and startles her back to the current moment.

"How did you sleep?" He asks quietly as his finger lingers on the top of her ear.

Her body shudders slightly as she refocuses her thoughts. "Fine."

Tristan's hand slides down to the back of her neck. "You ok today love?" He asks.

Calandra takes a deep breath, unsure of how to respond to that. *Sure, it's just that I had a vision of my dead mother drowning me in some horrible black lake and came back to reality just as I took my last breath.* She quickly decides that there is no sane response.

"Yeah." She pauses as she tries to plan the words in her head before she speaks them. "It's just- I had a daydream thing on the way here."

Tristan is aware of her experiences, as he has always chosen to call them out of respect for her hate of the word daydream. He's witnessed her having them numerous times. Tristan is the only one she feels she can really talk to about them. He is the only one who doesn't seem to think she's insane.

Calandra's dad had actually sent her to a couple different therapists over the years in hopes they would know how to 'fix' her. After the fourth one, Calandra gave in and began to pretend she didn't have them anymore. Whether Chase truly believes it or not, Calandra isn't sure of. One way or another, it is a subject neither of them brings up any longer.

Tristan, on the other hand, has never judged or treated her differently for them. He shows nothing but concern for her when she tells him about them. He's convinced that she actually has a spiritual gift of prophecy, but that she's fallen too far away from her beliefs for the gift to be able to function properly.

"You probably don't need to be driving." Tristan says as he squeezes gently at the base of her neck.

"I'm fine." She smiles reassuringly at him.

The sun starts to come over the horizon just barely. The clouds blend into multiple shades of pinks and purples. It's a beautiful morning. The temperature is nice and breezy even though it's so close to summer. Calandra knows this weather mixed with the scenery of the rising sun is exactly the kind of beautiful sight that will take her mind off of her daydream.

"How set are you on going to school today exactly?" She asks and gives him a slightly devious smile.

Tristan stares at her for a moment, not entirely sure if she's serious or not. "Why?" He draws out the word.

"I need a distraction, I need— I don't know I

need to get these images out of my head. And I know where to go to do it. Are you with me?" It rushes out of her mouth, each word trips over the next and forms a jumbled mess.

He gives her a look and slightly bites the left side of his bottom lip as he thinks about what to do. One of the quirks that she loves about him is the way he bites on his lip and twitches his head when he thinks. After a moment, he nods slightly and Calandra pulls off the road they're on and takes them back the opposite direction. She has never shared her favorite place with anyone before. The place that she goes to clear her mind and get away when she needs to. She had found it a few years ago. There's something about it that makes her feel alive. When she's there she feels like maybe, just maybe, there's something more out there waiting for her to discover it. She has no idea what that something may be, but something more nonetheless.

Calandra's dad is an uptight and very religious man. He raised her to be that way as well, but much to his disappointment, she hasn't quite become the girl he had hoped for yet. It's not that she doesn't believe in God, it's just that she still has questions. She has yet to have that breakthrough moment where God and all that comes with Him is just crystal clear. She's never had the point of grace that takes her from knowing who God is to having a relationship with Him, which has left her wondering if there is such a thing at all.

Her dad had been trying to force her into the experience for years, which hasn't helped to move anything along any quicker, much to his frustration. Tristan is quite religious as well. His parents are Christians, but they are not pushy about it like Calandra's father is. Being with Tristan and his family is actually a breath of fresh air for her, and she's come to enjoy being there even more than being at home, especially here of late.

At home she seems to do nothing but irritate and argue with her dad. He pushes the subject of religion and when she has no answers for him, it turns into a huge ordeal. She has found that no matter how complicated her dad makes things, when she's in her special place, things are different, things just seem right. She feels at peace there, she feels whole when she's out in nature. Suddenly, her nerves start to build at the thought of allowing someone else into an area that is so sacred to her. Her body tenses a little and Tristan feels it under his hand.

"Are you okay?" He asks nervously.

Calandra nods her head. "Yeah, just still a bit off I guess."

Feeling her anxiety, Tristan reaches with his other hand and turns the music back up. He knows how music comforts her. Calandra's nerves start to calm instantly. They pull into the driveway of Calandra's house and Tristan turns to her, confused.

Chapter 2
Trust

"Um, this is your special place?" He asks, slightly dumbfounded.

"No, not the house. Are you ready to explore?" She says more as a dare than a question.

Tristan nods and gets out of the car. He walks around and opens the door for Calandra.

Calandra had learned early on in their relationship that Tristan was raised to believe in chivalry. She wasn't allowed to open her door when he was here. The one time she had decided to open the door and get out on her own, he actually made her get back in and wait for him to do it. Most of the time, it actually seemed a bit ridiculous in her mind for her to have to wait, despite being perfectly capable of opening the door on her own. Regardless of her own opinion on the door ordeal, she knew it was important to him for whatever reason. Because of that she humors him with it. He wraps his hand tightly around hers and waits for Calandra to lead the way.

After walking a ways through the woods with no sign of stopping, Tristan stops and turns to Calandra. "So, what? You just happened to stumble into this place in the middle of the woods?" He asks with an eyebrow raised.

"No..." Calandra says as she looks at the ground. "I found a picture of my mom with her grandmother, and after a lot of coaxing, dad finally told me that it was from somewhere out here." She explains as she continues to look at the ground.

"And how long did it take you to find it?" Tristan asks as Calandra takes his hand and leads him down another winding path.

"Not long at all actually!" She smiles proudly. "I found it on my first shot thank you very much!" Calandra resists the urge to stick her tongue out, realizing just how childish it would be.

Tristan looks at her puzzled. "How exactly did you manage that?"

Calandra blushes and shrugs her shoulders. "We won't go there." She says simply and walks faster down the path that is growing more narrow and grown over. No matter how supportive and unjudgemental Tristan is about her experiences, she finds herself unable to tell him that a daydream of her mother is what led her to the place she now considers to be her sanctuary.

Tristan lets go of her hand and quits

walking. "Why is that?"

"I just—" Calandra isn't sure how to finish. "Come on, let's just keep going." She turns and starts walking again.

Tristan grabs her arm and stops her. He makes her turn to face him. He steps toward her and stands with his body just far enough from hers to not touch her. "Cal, what is it?" He asks.

"It's nothing." Tristan narrows his eyes at her to push her to tell him the truth. "It's just that you probably wouldn't believe me. I don't wanna talk about it." She hesitates between every word.

"Wouldn't believe what?" He runs a single finger down the side of her face.

She knows exactly where this is going to lead, so she quickly makes herself look down. Tristan's eyes have a hold on her, a control over her. He knows exactly how to break through her walls, and she isn't ready to let this one down yet, which means that she can't risk looking into his eyes. Tristan puts two fingers under her chin and tries to lift her face up to meet his. She pushes against it and leaves her gaze focused on the ground. Tristan brings his face next to hers, so they are cheek to cheek. His mouth rests just in front of hers, close enough she can feel the words he speaks land on her skin. He cups his left hand against the other side of her face gently. "You trust me right Cal?" He whispers softly.

Calandra's breath unsteadies and her heart jumps erratically in her chest. She feels as if she can't find enough air to talk, so she simply nods her head once against his face.

"Nothing you say is going to push me away." He speaks a bit louder this time, but draws the words out enough that they linger on her skin. "I love you and you can't change that no matter what. You don't have to tell me if you don't want to, but either way, I need you to believe that, ok?"

Calandra hadn't realized that her eyes closed. She breathes in through her nose to take in every detail of the moment. "Ok." She breathes out and the word rushes out faster than she had intended.

She feels Tristan's face slowly pull towards the front of hers, their skin brushes together as he does and she opens her eyes just as his eyes met hers. The world stops. Her heart suddenly has no rhythm to its beating. Her skin pulses. She looks deep into the baby blue oceans that stare back at her and nothing else matters anymore. She is safe, she can feel that. He is telling her the truth, she can see it; and she never wants to look away.

Tristan moves back further, still holding her gaze as he does. He smiles wickedly. He knows full well the control his gaze has over her. He takes her hand in his and runs his fingers slowly against her knuckles.

"So, shall we continue?" He asks. Calandra shakes herself out of the trance he's somewhat intentionally put her in and turns back towards the path deciding not to say anything. Tristan chuckles quietly as she takes him down the remainder of the pathway.

They turn down a few more small trails before coming to a patch of trees that stand out from the rest. They are oaks, just like the majority of the trees in the wood. But these are brighter, more vibrant, and the leaves are at least twice as big as the ones on the rest of the trees. Calandra stops and breathes in the air. The trees give off a musky, wood scent that somehow makes Calandra feel more alive. Calandra lets go of Tristan's hand and motions for him to follow her. The unique oaks start to thin out and get further apart from each other and eventually open up into a beautiful, randomly shaped, treeless area. Calandra immediately walks to the center of the area and lies down amongst the flowers. She closes her eyes, and exhales audibly as the remnants of the vision finally leave her.

    Tristan still stands at the opening as he takes in all the scenery. There are thousands of vibrant blue flowers that are unlike any he has seen before. They look like some type of lily, they cup at the bottom and then open up wide and invitingly at the top. The grass is greener than he knew was possible. But what really takes Tristan's breath away has nothing to do with the scenery.

    He's never seen Calandra look so peaceful. She lies in the grass with her eyes closed. She is relaxed and has the most serene look he's ever seen on a person on her face. Her hair is spread across the grass around her head in an unnaturally perfect way. The sun shines on her skin and makes it appear to have a slight glow. He walks slowly over to her and stands just beside her and looks down at her.

Calandra squints one eye open and sees Tristan smiling over her. "What do you think?" She asks quietly.

"I think you're breathtaking." He matches her volume and continues to stare without blinking.

Calandra giggles and blushes. "I meant what do you think of my little area here dear, but thank you."

Tristan kneels down next to her. "I'm serious Cal, this place brings something out in you. I've never seen you more beautiful than you are right now."

Calandra opens her eyes at that and small black dots catch her attention at the edges of her peripheral. As soon as she tries to focus, they dart off and out of her sight. Tristan's fingers lace into hers and a tingling sensation shoots through her. She closes her eyes again and takes comfort in the moment. The serenity of her favorite place mixes with Tristan's touch and makes the earlier experience seem as if it never happened.

Tristan lies down on his stomach beside her and props himself up with his left elbow. He slowly runs his fingers through her hair that's sprawled out on the ground in front of him. The air around them smells sweet. Calandra breathes it in slowly and relishes in the emotions it sends through her. She feels Tristan move her hair from in front of him. He stretches his arm out in front of him and lays his head on it as he faces her.

"I love you." He whispers softly in her ear, close enough she can feel the words touch her skin before she hears them. She smiles sweetly and tightens her grip on his hand. She feels his hand slowly brush her cheek. Tristan turns her face to the side to meet his. She feels his breath on her lips for several intoxicating moments before she opens her eyes. Tristan's lips meet hers and the world around her vanishes.

Chapter 3
Ruined

The sun slowly disappears into the horizon and turns the sky numerous shades of orange, pink, and blue. Tristan holds Calandra close, arm in arm, as they walk leisurely back through the woods. Neither of them can seem to fathom when enough time had passed for the sun to set. Calandra's mind is still fuzzy as they head back to her house. Her whole body feels lighter than usual. The blood seems to pulse through her veins with more energy than normal, and her smile has yet to falter. One of the many things she loves about her and Tristan's relationship is how good it feels to just be together. They don't have to do anything, most times they don't even talk. Some of her favorite times have been from just sitting with each other and enjoying being in each other's presence. Today had been one of those times of simply being together that she knows will be remembered as one of her favorite moments with Tristan.

She repositions her arm and unhooks it from Tristan's to hold his hand instead. She swings their arms enthusiastically as they walk and begins to hum lightly. Calandra notices Tristan's smile widen when he hears her start humming. She turns her head to give him a curious look, but trips over a branch in the path. Just before she hits the ground, she feels Tristan's arm wrap around her hip and pull her back onto her feet.

"Oops!" She chuckles.

Tristan laughs at the silly face she makes as she says it.

"At least I have someone to catch me."

Tristan's smile turns daring as he leans over and picks her up. He cradles her against his chest, with one arm at the small of her back and the other under her knees.

"Oh, and someone to carry me! That's even better!" Calandra wraps an arm around Tristan's neck and settles into his hold.

"Well I can't have you coming home cut and bruised. Chase wouldn't like that very much." He smiles.

Calandra scoffs at the mention of her dad. "At least he leaves tomorrow." She says as her smile fades a bit.

"Hmm, you're gonna need a big strong manly man to protect you this summer." He smiles. "Besides, you know you shouldn't be happy about your dad leaving the country for four months Cali."

Calandra rolls her eyes. "Where do you

suppose I could find one of those manly men?" She smiles and decides to ignore the last part of his statement.

Tristan isn't in anyway the guy that you would look at and think of the word manly or macho. He's too kind and gentle, and it always shows clear on his face, even if he tries to hide it. The wind rushes in and makes his hair swoop down over his eyes. As usual, he doesn't seem to care much, but Calandra sweeps the hair away to keep it from hiding his eyes. The smile that crosses his face as she does, makes her wonder if he actually left it there on purpose. Tristan is what Calandra refers to as an emo jock, which is of course a bit of a contradictory description, but it fits him perfectly.

Tristan scoffs as her comment hits him and he starts to drop her. Not wanting to let go she holds tightly to his neck, and hangs with her feet off the ground smiling innocently at him.

"Protect me from what anyways?" She asks. "The boogey man?

"CALANDRA!" Chase's voice booms from

the back porch.

Had it not been for him yelling at them, she wouldn't have noticed that they were out of the woods and in her back yard now. She immediately puts her feet on the ground and steps away from Tristan and turns to look at her dad. She wonders how long he's been standing there. If the look of anger on his face is any sign, he's seen more than enough.

"Yes father?" She responds, only slightly tinting the words with an attitude.

"Inside NOW!" Is all he says before he goes back into the house and slams the door behind him.

Calandra looks sheepishly at Tristan. "I could probably use some protection from that." She pouts.

Tristan cups her cheek in his hand. "I wish I could help you there babe. I'll catch a ride home from Phillip. Chase will only be worse on you if I come in." He gently brushes his lips against hers for a tender, all too short moment, then turns and walks away.

Phillip is Tristan's best friend, who conveniently enough lives across the street from Calandra. It was thanks to that convenience that Tristan and Calandra had met so many months ago. Phillip didn't like Calandra too much and because of that Tristan no longer goes over just to see him anymore. Ever since they started dating, Tristan always comes to Calandra's and then maybe stops by to visit Phillip before he goes home.

Calandra pouts for a moment before taking a few deep breaths to try and prepare for what is to come. She drags her feet as she walks into the house and shuts the door behind her. Chase is pacing a circle in the living room. Calandra looks at the ground as she walks to the couch to sit down. A few very awkward moments pass while she waits for her dad to say something, anything. "I've decided that you need to stay at your grandmother's while I'm gone." He finally says. He breathes heavily and his voice sounds a bit beyond hateful.

"Or not!" Calandra squeals.

"I'm sorry, I don't remember saying this was a discussion!"

"No, of course not! Nothing ever is when it comes to you dad!" Calandra yells as she stands up off the couch.

Calandra's grandmother, Chase's mom, Gwendyll, lives two states away in an uptight neighborhood. She's even worse than Chase, everything must be totally prim and proper and go by some sort of etiquette book that must've been written by an old woman who obviously had her Cheerio's peed in every day of her life. Calandra sometimes wonders if it was possibly even Gwendyll herself that wrote said book.

"I'm not getting into this with you. The decision is made and you leave tomorrow, end of discussion."

"Absolutely not!" Calandra says louder, and harsher than she intends. "I'm staying here, just like you said I could 6 months ago when you found out about your stupid trip!"

"That was before *him*." Chase says the last word with a few extra doses of hate.

Calandra rolls her eyes and stomps a foot on the ground. "His name is Tristan and I'm staying here."

"What?! So you can spend your whole summer running around with him and doing who knows what? I think not Calandra!"

"Yeah- that's exactly it dad!" Calandra scoffs. "You know if you took the time to actually get to know Tristan at all this wouldn't even need to be a discussion in the first place!" Calandra stomps up to her room.

She sits on her bed and crosses her legs in front of her. She holds back the tears that threaten to break through the tough, angry front she wants to wear. Calandra hears Chase pace the living room below her. He's trying to let his anger simmer down, but it usually just stews until it reaches its boiling point and then everything blows up in both of their faces.

Chase tends to act like Tristan is some disrespectful guy, probably because he never even put in an effort into finding out who Tristan really is. If only Chase knew that Tristan respects and holds the boundary line of their relationship up just as highly as she does, possibly even higher, then Chase might not have to worry so much about leaving. A blue dragonfly circles around her room and she finds the buzz from its little wings comforting.

The tears are just about to win the battle and break through when she hears Chase start to stomp up the stairs. She swallows the urge to cry, puts her angry front back on the best she can, and braces herself for what's about to come. Her door swings open and she immediately knows from the look on Chase's face that his anger certainly hasn't died down during his pacing and praying session.

"What are you doing up here?" She asks as hatefully as she can make it sound. "Get out of my room I just want to be-" She breaks off as she battles with the best way to finish the sentence. "I just want to be!"

"I won't stand idly by and let that boy take you down with him." He yells.

"Take me down? What are you even talking

about right now dad? The only place Tristan wants to take me is to church which should make you of all people happy!" She emphasizes the word dad and gives it a slight taste of disgust as she says it.

"He will destroy you Calandra. You may not know it, but I do! I know it all too well!"

The anger boils inside her, ready to explode. She tries to fight it back down, but it's no use. "What? You mean like you did mom?" She hadn't meant to say it, but there was no turning back now. She didn't even know why she said it. It wasn't like she actually knew anything about her mom, let alone the story behind their love. All she knows is what she has seen in her little daydreams, and after her latest one she really doesn't have the slightest idea of what to think of her mom.

Chase never talks about his relationship with her mom, or her death, or her at all really. It is a topic that is just never brought up. A topic that Calandra has always left buried away somewhere secret, until now. The curiosity burns inside her when she realizes, by the look on

Chase's face, that there must be some kind of truth in what she said. His skin turns blanket white, and his forehead is clammy. There's something in his eyes, something she's never seen before. Before she can try and figure out what it is, he blinks and it instantly switches back to anger.

"You know what Calandra? I'm done! You obviously have your mom and Echo in you even though I've tried to stomp it out." He stands there and stares at her.

"Why didn't you defend my claim to you ruining mom? What does that mean?" She squeaks out. She can't focus on anything other than the fact that he had said nothing to her accusation.

Chase turns and walks out the door. "You'll find out soon enough I suppose." He yells as he slams the door behind him.

The tears break through then, but they aren't just sad tears now. They are anger mixed with confusion, angst, betrayal, and desperation for answers. Before she knows what she's doing, Calandra finds herself throwing a duffle bag on her bed and she begins to fill it with clothes. She storms into her bathroom and fills her arms with hygiene necessities and jams them into the bag. She unplugs her phone charger from the wall and throws it in before she forces the zipper closed. She throws the bag over her shoulder and wipes the tears from her eyes.

    She stares at herself in the mirror on her vanity right next to her door. Her hair is blonde with small red and orange streaks throughout. She is slender and average height and her skin is on the extra pale side, which only makes her eyes stand out more than they already do. Her eyes are bright and tawny colored, what makes them more than a little unusual are the tiny streaks of orange in them. Calandra has never exactly fit into any category for looks. She's always stood out, which is what Tristan says makes her beautiful. But she doesn't buy into it, to her it just makes her a freak. Her face is currently red and puffy from crying, but there isn't anything she can do about that now, so she takes a few deep breaths and walks out of her room.

Without a second thought, she walks right past Chase, who is sitting on the couch, and she turns towards the front door. The hallway has never seemed as long before as it does at this moment. Calandra anticipates the noise of Chase's footsteps behind her before she actually hears them. "Just go away dad!" Calandra sucks up her tears and refuses to let her voice break as she says it. "I don't want to talk, I just want to go."

"Go where?" He yells.

"What do you care?"

"You are still my responsibility!" Chase hesitates before he says it, cutting the knife even further into Calandra's chest.

"Are you going to tell me what your silence up there meant about Mom?" The tears become harder to hold back and Calandra knows she has to wrap up and leave or she won't be able to hold them off any longer.

Chase stares back at her blankly. He opens his mouth, but closes it again before any words make it out. He looks down at the ground and turns and walks back down the hall.

Calandra's eyes sting against the tears as she turns to watch him walk away. "So that's it?!" She asks mixing her shock and hurt into her tone.

"You're asking questions you probably don't actually want to know the answers to Calandra. Despite what you may want to believe, a lot of times, the truth has a tendency to hurt." He says as he walks the rest of the way down the hall and leaves her standing at the door alone.

"So what, I guess that means that lies are beautiful?" She sighs as the tears break through and she walks out the door.

She jogs to her car, unsure of why she's in such a hurry. She has a feeling Chase isn't going to come after her regardless. Her heart races, and the adrenaline pumps through her veins. Her head is throbbing, her eyelids feel like they are on fire from the stinging tears that stream down her face. The tears blur in the corners of her eyes and she has to blink rapidly to clear her vision as she makes her way to the car.

Her phone still sits in the middle console of her car from the drive that morning. She picks it up and pushes the unlock button. There's a message waiting from Tristan.

You doing ok Cal?

Calandra smiles for the first time since before Tristan left her and she types a quick response.

I will be, once I see you. It was worse than usual, I'm leaving now.

She wipes her eyes once more and turns on her car. Her radio had been left turned up too loud and the sudden noise makes her jump. She turns the radio off instantly and pulls out of the driveway. With her car in the road, just next to her driveway, she takes one last deep breath. She looks up to the house once more and her heart breaks again when she sees her father hasn't made the effort to come out for her. She sighs and drives away from her house.

The thoughts pound away. The vibration of the car, the soft humming of the engine, the random bumps in the road. Everything combines and makes the wheels in her head turn faster than they ever have before. Why couldn't he have just come out again? She feels as if she can't keep up with herself. She tries to focus on the cars as they pass by and hopes the light will blind everything else out of her head.

Just as her head finally starts to clear, the cars quit coming. She's alone on the road. The night fills the world around her as she starts down a stretch of road with mostly trees and only a few houses scattered in. The thoughts threaten to flood back in, and she fights against it. Calandra reaches down to turn the radio back on in hopes the music will kill her last few lingering thoughts.

Calandra manages to calm her shakes and her limbs that can't seem to stay still enough to keep the car moving and on the road. She spends most of the drive to Tristan's house in an effort to calm herself and ignore the thoughts echoing in her head. It feels like an eternity before she makes it to Tristan's, and she finds him standing in the driveway, waiting for her arrival. He is at the car before she's able to turn off the engine. He opens the door and pops his head inside the door instantly.

"Are you okay Cal?" He asks sincerely.

Calandra tries, but she can't seem to make herself say anything, she simply stares at him. The beauty of his eyes overtakes her, and for once, she doesn't fight the urge to get lost in them. Being lost is all she wants at this point. She is broken, more so than she usually is after an argument with her dad, but then again he's also never actually let her leave before.

"Cal, you're shaking." Tristan reaches over her and takes the keys out of the ignition. He grabs her bag from the passenger seat and gently brings it over her, careful not to hit her as he does so. Calandra still sits frozen and stares at him. Tristan puts her bag on his shoulder, reaches his arm around Calandra's back, and pulls her out of the car gently.

Calandra slightly pulls out of her daze long enough to allow him to help her out of the car. Her head is clouded in thoughts and pictures of the fight. She is in a state of mind that will hardly allow her to move. She feels completely exasperated and like she isn't really here, as if she is somewhere else entirely and in a way she wishes she was. Calandra tries to help Tristan walk her into the house, but she isn't very successful in doing so and she practically just leans into him while he does all the work. Out of the corner of her eyes, she sees Tristan's parents in the doorway as they walk in. His mom opens her mouth to say something, but Tristan waves her off before any words make it out.

"She's ok, she just needs to get away from him for a bit. I'm going to get her situated in my room and I'll come back down and sleep on the couch. We'll talk then." He whispers even though Calandra can hear every word he says.

Tristan's mom nods and his parents disappear into the living room. Tristan smiles reassuringly at Calandra. "Let's get you laying down ok? You'll feel better after you get some sleep." Without waiting for a response, he leads her up the stairs to his room.

Tristan gently lowers Calandra's body on the bed, he lays her bags on the floor next to the end table and crawls into bed next to her. He scoots his body directly next to hers and wraps his arm around her. Calandra feels like a zombie. Her head is pounding and the thoughts feel as if they are trying to beat their way out of her skull. She tries a few times to talk, to explain to Tristan what's wrong, but nothing comes out.

"We can talk about it later. For now, just get some rest." Tristan whispers and he pulls her head into his chest.

Relieved for the first time of the night, Calandra breaths in his scent. She washes out her mind the best she can, and lets the tears flow freely into Tristan's chest while he runs his fingers gently through her hair until she finally passes out.

LAINY LANE

Chapter 4
No Apology

Calandra awakes to find herself alone in Tristan's room. Not that she expected any less, but it doesn't stop the loneliness from creeping in and filling her with dread. Its only a few moments before her mind clears enough for her to register where Tristan should be; downstairs sleeping on the couch. This wasn't the first time her and

Chase had gotten into a fight bad enough for her to leave and look for a place to stay for the night. Tristan always gave up his bed when she needed it and he slept on the couch. Calandra had a feeling his parents probably didn't actually sleep on those nights, but they would never turn her away.

There have certainly been plenty of times that Calandra finds herself wishing she had a family more like Tristan's. They are what you could call the All-American dream family, like Leave it to Beaver or The Walton's, but for modern day. Tristan's dad, Kyle, works for a decent sized corporation in their IT department doing something Calandra can't even begin to understand. Trisha, Tristan's mother, is a stay at home mom and has always been involved in Tristan's school and extra curricular activities. Currently, she is the mother that always brings the fun snacks to football practices and games, all of the players call her mom. Kyle and Trisha don't have any children other than Tristan, and though Calandra doesn't know the exact details behind why, she is quite certain judging by their personalities that it wasn't a choice they had made to only have one child.

Tristan has never wanted for anything, other than maybe to sleep in every once in a while. This household was the kind of house that everyone was up by seven am, regardless of what day it is. That was the only thing that Calandra really hated about being here, they didn't seem to believe in sleeping in for some reason. If her and Tristan did end up getting married one day, that was going to have to be the first thing she instilled in him.

The Victorian style house is filled with pictures of Tristan, he was their pride and joy, and they weren't ashamed to show it. Their family went to church every Sunday, but unlike Calandra's father, they raised Tristan without spite. Spite was what Calandra felt her father used when it came to dealing with her. She has always wondered if Chase blamed Calandra for her mother, Hollyn, being gone now. He hadn't exactly signed up or been in the least bit prepared to be a single father, at least that was the defense Tristan always brought to her attention when things got rough between them.

Calandra stretches every limb as far as she can as she tries to convince herself to get out of bed and head downstairs. The scent of bacon and eggs coming from the kitchen should be more than enough to entice her lazy butt to crawl down there and act like something a little more coherent than a zombie, but her body wasn't entirely convinced yet. Her stomach was willing but the rest of her was still debating whether or not it was really worth the effort required. Her head felt groggy and clouded as she willed herself to sit up. She felt top heavy and for a few moments she thought she might actually fall forward in the bed. She closed her eyes and puts her head in her hands and massages her temples in hopes that her head will unfuzz enough to function the least little bit.

"Oh good, you're awake." Tristan's voice is always way too cheerful first thing in the morning, Calandra has never understood how that happens as she is the furthest thing from a morning person. Tristan walks in with a silver tray in hand and a plethora of breakfast foods and juices spread across it.

"I take it there was probably a debate going on downstairs as to whether or not I was alive just yet."

"Always is when you stay the night." Tristan chuckles. "You know us crazy morning people don't fully understand you afternoon people!"

"Like you said, y'all are the crazy ones." Calandra's voice is still scratchy from just waking up and her esophagus burns a bit as she speaks.

"How are you feeling today babe?" Tristan sets the tray of food on the bed before her and takes a seat across from her where he begins to thoroughly study her for any sign of demise.

This is the normal routine after she gets into a fight with her dad. She's been through it enough times to know what every step of the 'feel better Cal' process is. It all starts with breakfast, which was Calandra's favorite part of the entire ordeal since Chase isn't much of a cook. Step two is the slightly annoying study of her movements as she eats incorporated with a game of twenty questions to check on her emotional stability. Once that was over, he would give her enough space to allow her to get ready, then the 'let me know if you need anything, you know I'll be there in an instant' speech would happen before she was allowed to leave. Tristan's parents would stay quiet and off to the side and do nothing more than give her sympathetic apology faces as she walked out of the house.

The entire process took less time than usual today and Calandra finds herself in her car with the music turned up and the windows rolled down before she knows it. The going back home and apologizing was the part that she always seemed to dread the most. It was usually worse than the fight was, mainly because of the anticipation of it. At least when they got into fights, no matter how bad they ended up, there was no time for her to work up her nerves before it happened. The apology and return part of the process was another story. She had the entire fifteen minute drive from Tristan's house to hers to do nothing other than mull over how mad Chase would be when she got there, how she would attempt to word the conversation, and ways to keep it all from leading to another argument, which would land her back into square one all over again.

Calandra pulls into the driveway with her heart racing and on the verge of having a full on anxiety attack, which is normally a good time to have Tristan around, but he always sent her for the big return alone. It was something she had to do on her own, according to him. Calandra lingers at the front door with her hand on the knob for a minute before gathering enough nerve to turn the knob and walk into the house.

"Dad?" She calls out with her voice laced with an apologetic tone.

No response. He was probably upstairs packing for his trip and distracted. He always waited until the very last second to pack for his trips, which led to way more stress than he ever seemed to actually know what to do with. Calandra walks over to the stairs and calls out for him up the stairs. Still nothing.

"Hmm." She sighs as she walks into the dining room to put her things down.

Just as she drops he bags onto the table, the yellow piece of notepaper catches her eye. It is covered in the scraggily handwriting that Calandra instantly recognizes as her father's.

Calandra,

There was an issue with my previous flight arrangements. To prevent having to travel in Coach, I had to reschedule things and take an earlier flight out. I cancelled your arrangements to go to your grandmother's as you obviously won't go anyways. There is money in the flour jar in the kitchen for while I am gone. Your grandmother has more stashed away if that isn't enough to get you by, though I trust that it should be.

No boys are allowed at the house while I am gone. You may have girlfriends over, but no more than three at a time. No parties! No

drinking! No making out with anyone! If you wouldn't do it while I'm here, then don't do it while I'm gone either! Call your grandmother if you need anything. I'll call you once I'm settled in and have a few minutes.

See you in a few months,

Chase

She drops the note out of her hand and watches as it flits back and forth a few times before landing back on the table where she had found it to begin with. She probably should've felt relieved that she didn't have to go through the normal apologizing routine. Instead she feels hurt and betrayed as the information sinks in. Her father had left without saying goodbye. Worse than that, he hadn't even attempted to apologize or seem the least bit regretful for the fight in the short and sweet note he had left for her.

Without fully recognizing what she is even doing, she immediately gets her phone out of her purse and dials Tristan's number.

"Everything okay Cal?" His voice is concerned when he answers.

"He left." Calandra's answer is vague and she doesn't clarify anything.

"Who left?"

"My dad. There's a goodbye note on the table, he went to his business project."

"Really?" For some reason, Tristan sounds pretty shocked.

"Yeah."

"Do you want me to come and get you?"

"No," Calandra replies, "I'm gonna go walk in the woods for a bit to clear my head. I'll let you know what I'm gonna do when I get back."

"Ok, be careful please."

"I will." She answers simply.

Calandra hangs up without saying goodbye and immediately knows she will hear about that decision the next time she sees Tristan. He has a thing with people who hang up without saying goodbye and she's never done it to him before. She shrugs her shoulders, tosses the phone on the table, and walks out the back door and heads for the woods.

Chapter 5
Secrets

Calandra walks through the woods, down the path she knows so well, towards her sanctuary. This has all been far too much for her lately. She needs peace, and her favorite place to find it is the sanctuary. Serenity comes easily as she walks down the winding pathways, she knows the clearing is soon coming where she will enter her spot of belonging. She can see the flowers in her head already, smell the soft fragrance that always makes her feel lighter. Her anticipation builds as she walks. She knows exactly where to dodge thorns and branches that stick out, she could make this journey in her sleep.

Her heart jumps when she sees the clearing. She ducks under the vines between the last trees to the opening, and enters her beautiful spot. Her breath catches as she feels all the stress of the world melt away from her. Nothing exists beyond the beauty of this place. She always feels better when she's here; more powerful and like anything is possible. She walks over to her favorite spot and lays down, ready to relax, close her eyes, and shut out the world completely. A soft noise distracts her; a hum, or maybe a soft buzz. Something blue catches her eye from somewhere to her back side. She turns to see what it is, and finds a beautiful blue and purple dragonfly.

"Why hello." She says quietly. "Would you like to join me?"

As if it understands exactly what she said, the dragonfly flies over and softly perches on her left shoulder, angling its body towards her face. It's tiny feet tickle her shoulder as it sits there. It's soft buzz fills her ears and she finds it oddly soothing. She smiles as she slowly and smoothly lies down, careful not to scare away her new friend. Her cares and worries disappear as she closes her eyes and lets her haven wash over her. The soft buzz soothes her as she feels the sense of belonging encase her. Safe in the surroundings of this special place she relaxes her entire being; her mind, body, and soul.

The dragonfly that's on her shoulder now seems to buzz louder, which alarms Calandra. She sits up, careful to not move as fast as she wants to, to keep from frightening her little watcher. Something catches her eye despite the shock of the sunlight that pierces her eyesight momentarily; a spear of light. A white all-encompassing light orb heads away from her. It moves slightly away from her, and stops, as if it is waiting for her to follow. Calandra isn't sure how she knows it wants her to follow it, but she can sense somehow that it is calling her towards it with its motions.

Her watcher buzzes steadily in her ear, which somehow eases her nerves away. Calandra takes the change in its noise as a safety assurance, and she carefully gets to her feet and cautiously follows after the light. The buzz from the dragonfly grows slightly and breaks Calandra from the daze of staring at the light. She picks her feet up off the ground, and continues to walk after the light. It takes a conscience effort on her part to remind herself to take each step because she is so enveloped in the beauty of the light.

She was obviously right in thinking the light wanted her to follow it, because as soon as she walks towards it, the light moves further forward. It waits for her to walk and then moves slightly ahead. It stops and waits for Calandra to catch up if she isn't right behind it, and then moves ahead further. They are going to the other side of the opening that Calandra calls her sanctuary, the side that she has never examined for some reason. There are a growing number of flowers as they reach the edge of the opening.

Calandra is unsure of what made her think that the light was going to stop instead of going through the edge of the clearing and into whatever lies on the other side, but she gasps audibly when she sees it disappear into the other side of the trees. She basks in the comfort of the buzzing coming from her shoulder. She takes a breath and walks through to the other side of the clearing. She hears water as soon as she breaks through. It is a soft babble, which she knows has to be coming from a creek.

She notices a figure on the other side of the creek. It is a man. He is tall and slender, with long hair in a style that certainly isn't from this century, or any other century that Calandra knows of. Somewhere deep down, Calandra knows that when you see a random guy in the woods- the best idea is probably to run the other way. Somehow that thought never crosses her mind as being a real possibility. The buzz on her shoulder slowly grows louder and encourages her even more towards her next move.

Calandra pulls her legs of her pants up slightly, so they won't catch as she dodges tree limbs and obstacles in the path that leads to the creek. She gets to the creek and into it without any issues. But as she stands in it, she realizes the incline to get back out of it isn't going to be anywhere near as easy to tackle. The water rushes around her bare feet and splashes onto her legs. The air is crisp and smells clean. All the while, the man just stares at her, he watches her every move with intrigue.

At least Calandra hopes it's intrigue and not some sort of fantastically disgusting creeper look. That's when Calandra realizes that she is far enough into the woods that no one can hear her scream, if she were to, for some reason, feel the need to do so. Her heart starts to race and she considers for a half a second whether or not she needs to turn around. She knows it's too late now, even if it is the smarter idea.

Just when she begins to think that turning around is in fact the best thing to do, the stranger cocks his head at her, and she catches a glimpse of his eyes. All her fears slip away instantly. She feels trapped in his sight, and even if she wanted to, she knows she can't turn back now. She feels drawn in, no matter what her inhibitions tell her she should do.

She grimaces as she walks over the stones at the bottom of the creek. They are all rather smooth, yet still slightly uncomfortable on her bare feet. She seems to cross the creek much faster than she should be able to, though she doesn't pay much attention to the act of walking across. She doesn't take her eyes off of the stranger the entire time. She isn't fully aware that she's on the other side until he reaches out to help her up the embankment to where he is. She takes his hand and allows him to help pull her up.

The stranger is tall and lean. His hair is a dark shade of blonde, with brown undertones in it. It comes down to just past his shoulders, where it lays quite untidily. There's a shorter layer that comes just past his ears, and side sweeping bangs that hang just past his eyebrows and cover his eyes slightly. The eyes that are slightly hidden under those bangs are the most gorgeous things Calandra has ever seen. They are an amazing color of baby blue with a slight tinge of teal. They're opaque, and seem to have a white tint to them. Calandra knows she could stare at them forever, if she were to allow herself to, so she immediately forces herself look away and distracts herself by taking in his outfit.

Calandra has never seen anything quite like what he's wearing. It's a bit out of the ordinary to say the very least. It's a mix of leather, frills, ruffles, boots, and there's even a little hint of glitter. Yet somehow, the odd mixture looks completely flawless on such a handsome person. The stranger is intriguing, mysterious, and beyond beautiful. Something about him draws her in and she can't seem to take her eyes off of him. Calandra doesn't think she'll ever be able to make herself quit staring at him. That's when she remembers that she still isn't totally sure if this stranger is going to attack her or possibly something even worse. The thought makes her heart beat irrationally and she starts planning a possible route of escape, just in case she decides she does indeed need to run off somewhere.

"I apologize for my rudeness." The stranger says and his voice is laced with honey. "I was just taken aback I guess. I'm Jarreth, it's nice to meet you Calandra."

Calandra stares even harder at him now. She hasn't been able to make herself speak yet, and somehow he knows her name. This certainly isn't working to calm her nerves any. She thinks harder on an escape plan, and starts to wander if she should already be running away.

"How do you know my name?" She finally makes herself ask.

"I know much more about you than you think." He holds his arm out towards her, as if to shake hers.

Calandra simply stares at it, unwilling to take it. He must catch onto this because he decides to give up on the gesture. He now reaches out to her shoulder and she feels two of his fingers rest gently on her exposed shoulder. She tingles from where his touch is all the way down to her toes. The sensation is somehow warm and cool at the same time. Calandra looks over at his fingers as they touch her skin. The dragonfly that she had all but forgotten was there slowly walks over to Jarreth's fingers and perches itself on them.

"Like, for instance, why this creature has decided to show a favoritism to you." Jarreth winks as he lifts his hand from her shoulder and the dragonfly leaves Calandra with it. He brings it just a few inches from his face and stares at it momentarily before he motions for it to fly on.

Calandra finally takes her eyes off of Jarreth long enough to watch the dragonfly slowly but gracefully fly away. When she quits watching the dragonfly, she realizes Jarreth is now staring at her. Calandra leans up against the tree behind her. She puts her hands directly against it and behind her back. She lifts one leg onto the tree trunk so, if she does feel the need to bolt, she can easily propel herself into the run. She feels like she should be scared, yet something about his eyes won't let her be.

"And just what exactly do you know about me?" She asks.

"I know everything your dad won't tell you, plus some." He answers with a soft chuckle.

Calandra stares at him blankly, her mouth is open slightly. This meeting certainly isn't getting any less awkward. "How could you possibly know that?"

He ignores her question and continues as if she hasn't said anything. "I also know that you feel like you're destined for something more, something bigger and better. I know why you feel that, and I can show you." He winks and turns and walks a few feet away. When he realizes she isn't following him, he stops and turns back to face her. He reaches out his hand. "Coming?" He asks with a smile.

Something tells Calandra she should run now. Somewhere inside of her she knows that following some random stranger who appears to belong to another century, and knows things he shouldn't know about you- things you don't even know- probably isn't the brightest of ideas. This remains true no matter how gorgeous his eyes may be. But even if she actually wanted to run, she still couldn't have made herself. She is hooked by intrigue and curiosity now. Calandra keeps a cautious look on her face, she pushes herself off of the tree and walks over to him.

Even though the thought crosses her mind and it is very tempting, she does make herself refuse his hand. Instead she simply motions in front of him. "Lead the way." She tells him instead.

He smirks and reaches down and takes her hand in his anyways before he begins walking. The tingling goes back through her, about a thousand times stronger this time. Heat fills her hand where he's holding her, but a cold chills fill the rest of her body. She tenses up from the feelings, but can't make herself pull away from him, so she takes a breath and follows him instead.

They walk through a winding trail along the creek before they come to a wall of ivy. Jarreth stops abruptly. Calandra's body fills with anxiety as they stand there holding hands. Jarreth turns to her without letting go of her. "Are you ready?" He asks with an odd twinkle in his eye.

Calandra shrugs, unsure of what she's supposed to be ready for.

Jarreth reaches out with his free hand and pulls part of the ivy wall back that creates an opening for them to walk through. "Ladies first my dear." He says as he lets go of her hand and motions for her to enter.

Calandra looks at him cautiously before she walks through. She has to remind herself to breathe once she takes a look around. She thought her sanctuary was breathtaking, but this takes beauty to a whole other level. Plush grass fills the small opening and it is littered with beautiful pink and blue flowers. The flowers are long and cylinder shaped. They face upward, with an opening at the top, and have a small heart shaped lid. The air is filled with a mixture of lily, pine, cedar, and something musky; it's an intoxicating combination of fragrances.

"This is the Field of Innocence." Jarreth says, answering the question she hasn't been able to form yet.

Calandra turns and looks at him. "Which is—" She prods for more information as she continues to take in the scenery.

"Just sit down and take it in for a minute." He says as he holds out a hand to assist her to the ground.

Calandra stares cautiously at him momentarily, but she can't make herself feel even the least bit threatened even though she tries. She sighs and takes his hand and allows him to help her sit down. She crosses her legs in the grass and inhales deeply to take in the scent. Something fills her as she does; a sense of belonging, tranquility, and true happiness. She opens her eyes back up to see the air around her has filled with dragonflies.

Suddenly she finds her thoughts swirling to visions of her mom and her great-grandmother. Her heart races momentarily, but a calm immediately rushes over her before her anxiety gets very high. Calandra looks up suspiciously at Jarreth, who smiles down at her. He nods knowingly before he slowly sits down beside her.

"Would you really like to know what your father won't tell you?" He asks sincerely with a tint of concern behind the words.

Calandra nods instantly, unable to feel nervous about it, even though she suspects she probably should.

Jarreth looks as if he is about to speak, but then stops. He takes in a quick breath before he takes Calandra's hand in his. Her heart starts to race. "Are you sure Cal? Please keep in mind that the truth isn't always pretty." His words take Calandra back to the night of her fight with her dad, just before she drove away from the house.

"And lies are beautiful." She repeats words similar to the ones she had said when her dad had spoke the all too similar line to her that night.

"Sometimes, yes." Jarreth replies.

Calandra's heart still beats all too fast and heat rises in her cheeks. She isn't sure what he can possibly tell her to make her hate her father anymore than she already does at the moment. She is already beyond hurt that he left town without even saying goodbye. She takes one last deep breath to ready herself for whatever is about to come. She nods her head to indicate to Jarreth that she does indeed want the truth.

"Please bear in mind Cal that your dad, in his own kind of way, thinks he is doing what is right— I guess." Jarreth squeezes her hand as he says it.

Calandra had forgotten that his hand was there, and suddenly being aware of it makes it feel awkward and wrong. She jerks away immediately and places her hands in her lap as she looks away from him. A sound comes out of Jarreth's mouth, Calandra is pretty sure it's a laugh of some sort, but she ignores it as he begins his story.

"Did you know that dragonflies are the faeries of the mortal earth?" Jarreth asks as if this were common knowledge.

Calandra shoots him a confused look and slightly shakes her head no, unsure of where this is supposed to be going.

"Dragonflies are the only of the Fae that can freely roam the mortal earth, with the exception of a few special places that other faeries are allowed to be."

Calandra looks around and before she can form the obvious question she wants to ask, he continues.

"Yes, here would be one of those places. The field of innocence is one of the few places we are allowed to freely roam. Your destiny started in this very place, long before you were ever actually thought of Calandra."

Every new thing he says makes Calandra think she should second-guess him, or at least have some sort of reaction. But truthfully she just feels numb.

"Your mother loved this place as well, for the same reasons that you found and love your sanctuary. She came back to here enough that she eventually saw a faerie coming in through that ring over there." Jarreth points behind him.

Calandra looks around him to see what he's

referring to. She's unsure of how she didn't notice it before. Just 15 feet from where they sit is a ring of mushrooms that range from red to blue and just inside of it is another ring of blue, purple, and pink wild flowers. The inside of the circle is lush green grass. On the outside of the ring of mushrooms are perfectly round and evenly spaced patches of dead grass. Surely it's the way the sun is shining, but Calandra swears there's a glow coming from the inside of it.

"Coming through as in—" Calandra can't process the thoughts in her head, she can't make the words come together and make sense, and she can't quit staring at the ring.

"Yes Cal, as in entering your world from ours. Your mother hid when she saw it, waited until he came back, watched him use the ring to cross back over, and followed after him." He explains.

Calandra's mouth drops open. "She entered into Faerie? Is that possible?"

Jarreth smiles. "That's just it dear, it isn't possible for a mortal to enter in without being accompanied by a Fae. But your mother, as it turns out, had a heritage that had been hidden from her, much as yours has. She stayed in our world for quite some time and learned about herself and her family."

Calandra's heartbeat races again, but only momentarily as her brain processes what he's saying. Her eyes widen once she pieces it together.

"So, my mom is a faerie?" She asks.

"Not full Fae, but she has faerie in her, yes." Jarreth smiles. "Your great grandmother had hoped that by living here in the mortal world, her family would be able have a normal life. But it wasn't possible for your mom to do so being that her soul was connected to our world. It's where she decided she wanted to be, without even realizing it. Much as your soul is."

It finally dawns on Calandra that Jarreth isn't only explaining that her mother had been partially faerie, but that she is as well. According to him, subconsciously she's been seeking this place all along. She's been trying to find Faerie without even realizing it. "And my dad knows?" She asks quietly.

Jarreth's eyes look sad and sympathetic. "Yes." He says simply. "Your dad knows a lot that he isn't telling you dear."

The better sense inside of her is telling her that she shouldn't believe him. She knows this all sounds straight out of some kind of fairy tale, literally. If the encounter had taken place a few days ago, she would've immediately written the ordeal off as some crazy hallucination. As it stands now, after the odd experience of her mother drowning her and her father obviously hiding something about his past with her mother, she finds herself intrigued in the idea of what the stranger is telling her.

"And how do you fit into this story exactly?" Calandra speaks the question before she realizes how rude it sounds.

Jarreth doesn't seem affected by it in the least. "I am simply ensuring that you find your destiny Calandra. You are tied to Faerie whether you want to be or not, that's where your destiny lies."

"Why should I believe any of this?" She is careful to word the question in a way to not imply that she doesn't have much doubt in his story.

"The beauty of the field of innocence, my dear, is that it is Fae enough to make all of the facades that your world tries to push on you disappear. When you're here, you're back to the innocence of a child. Ridden of all the untruths your people have made up over the years, and free to see things for what they really are. You believe because of where you are, because this place makes you feel that it is real. You believe because you are linked to it— in here." Jarreth places his hand over her heart.

She suddenly has a comfort wash over her as he stares intently at her. It seems like an eternity passes as they sit and stare at each other. All at once, he pulls away from her, and she finds there is a painful absence from him doing so. Jarreth stands up and holds his hand out as if to help her up as well. She takes it and backs away from him once they are up off the ground.

"How are you doing Cal?" He asks her though he still won't look at her.

"Does the truth always have to hurt?" She asks.

"Usually, yes."

Calandra nods her head and looks down at the ground. "Figures. I guess I should've kept dealing with the lies and just left well enough alone."

He places one hand on her cheek, and shakes his head at her. "No dear, not all lies are beautiful. And who's to say the truth can't hurt at first, but still turn into something amazing in the end? You never know what you could turn out to be if you just hold on." Jarreth smiles, winks, and slowly removes his hand from her face and walks away which leaves her with a desire for so much more than what he gave. Jarreth steps into the ring and with a flash of light disappears in front of her very eyes. Calandra collapses onto the ground.

Chapter 6
Purpose

Calandra had said that she wanted to be alone and Tristan knew exactly where that meant she was going. At first, Tristan was planning on letting Calandra have her time alone. That theory ended when she hung up the phone without saying goodbye. With that simple action, she had given away just how upset she really was. Tristan had immediately left the house and headed to hers. He had no idea what to expect and was unsure of what kind of state he would find her in. He didn't need to go into the house, because he knew exactly where she would be. She needed to go to the woods to think. He quickly thanked God for her showing him the place she went to think just the day before. He knew exactly where to find her.

When he broke through to her sanctuary, he was left completely breathless. What seemed to be a million dragonflies were flying around the field. They were all blues and purples in color. They gracefully flew in no particular pattern around her. She was lying in the middle of the field on her back to watch them. Calandra seemed especially mesmerized by them. Calandra seemed to be in a daze. She wasn't looking away from the dragonflies. Tristan slowly walked over to her, careful not to make much noise as he went. She looked so peaceful and relaxed, he didn't want to disturb her.

"Have you ever really noticed dragonflies

and what amazing creatures they are?" Calandra didn't acknowledge Tristan's presence until she spoke.

"Why do you say that Cal?" Tristan asks as he takes a seat next to her and gently runs a hand through her hair that is sprawled out on the grass beneath her.

"Think about it, have you ever seen any other animal or creature with the flight pattern they have? It's so uncalculated, they pause every few inches with a sudden jolt, only to continue along where they were already headed to begin with." She explains as she continues to stare at the dragonflies.

"Seems like that would make them kind of stupid, not amazing, wouldn't it?" He responds.

At that she over looks at him. "Why would you say that?" she snaps.

"Well why would you want to waste the gift of flight like that? I mean think how quickly they could get where they were going if they just flew straight there instead of acting all ADD as they go." He sounds more defensive than he means to.

"That's just what makes them amazing though. Don't you see Tristan?" She turns her gaze back to the dragonflies around them before she continues. "They don't rush through everything like humans do. They see the beauty in the world, and they savor it. They stop to take in every moment, every inch of the world around them. They study their surroundings, appreciate the things that we always take for granted from day to day. Maybe that's why they were given wings to fly and we weren't, cause we wouldn't truly appreciate the gift. We'd just use it to make everything go faster like we try to do with everything else."

Tristan watches her as she speaks passionately about something he doesn't think should matter very much. Every few seconds a dragonfly perches on her somewhere, whether it's on her arm, her shoulder, or her knee, one even lands square on her nose. None of them ever land on him, even though he's being stiller than she is. She keeps reaching her hands into the air in an attempt to touch one, they glide over her finger when she does and each time her smile brightens. Tristan simply watches her in amazement and continues smiling down at her.

"That's why I love you." He says as he rakes his fingers through her hair.

"Because I love dragonflies?"

"No," he laughs, "because of your passion for things, even when they are things that no one else would ever notice."

"So you love my weirdness?" She smiles goofily up at him.

"Yes Cal, I do." He chuckles as he leans into her and kisses her gently.

"It would make sense you know." She says and goes back to watching the dragonflies as if nothing had happened.

"My love for you or did you just go down a whole different path on me?" Tristan asks.

"Oh no, sorry," Calandra giggles, "the dragonflies being the faeries of this world." She sits up as she says it and several dragonflies land on various places on her.

"What exactly are you talking about dear?"

Tristan watches her carefully. She seems to glow as she watches the dragonflies interact with her.

It suddenly hits Calandra that she hasn't told him anything about the experience, or meeting, with Jarreth that she had before he arrived. She was still pretty confused on what had happened herself. She could remember meeting Jarreth, he showed her a new area of the woods she had never seen before, he told her things about her father and dragonflies, and then he disappeared. Literally, he had disappeared into a ray of light. Calandra couldn't remember anything after that really. She had blacked out after Jarreth evaporated into thin air. She awoke to dragonflies everywhere and she was back in her favorite little place. A part of her was wondering if it was some sort of dream. But she didn't remember falling asleep beforehand. Her head was starting to feel like a pressure cooker.

"Cal?" Tristan pulls her out of her thoughts.

"Yes dear?" She answers him without fully paying attention to him.

"Are you ok?" He leans over to get a better

look at her and gives her a once over, looking for any sign of distress.

"I'm fine, I just— I had a daydream thing before you got here... I think."

"You think?" Tristan was lost and worried at this point.

"Yeah, I mean, it didn't seem like a daydream, it seemed real, more real than usual. But, I don't know—" None of it made enough sense to be able to form into a logical statement. Tristan looked at her questioningly. Calandra quickly explained the entire ordeal in completely vague and no more coherent sentences. Her head started running together and her thoughts were having head on collisions with each other as she spoke.

"So, what would that make you exactly... if this were real?"

"Hypothetically you mean?" Calandra interjected with a tinge of offense in her voice.

Tristan nods in agreement.

"I don't know what it makes me Tristan," she sighs, "but I do intend to find out if this is all real and, if so, what it means exactly."

What she has never told Tristan, in a completely open and totally truthful manner, are the questions that have always filled her about the world and religion. She has tried to grow closer to Tristan by being involved in the church. Before Tristan, church was something she had begun pulling away from because of her father and the wounded relationship she had with him. She wanted to change that, for Tristan, but no matter how hard she tried to change for him, it just didn't feel right deep down in her gut.

Her family obviously had some kind of hidden secrets that her father would never be ready to discuss. She would, of course, like to believe that there was something else out there, something more than what she saw from day to day in the world. She would love to discover that life had more meaning, more beauty, and more purpose to it than the nonchalantness she found in her home living with Chase. Everything Jarreth had told her fit right in with all of her lifelong fantasies. So it made sense for it to be real, right?

Calandra pulls her knees into her chest and wraps her arms around them and puts her chin into her knees. She stares in the direction the light had taken her to met Jarreth before. She sighs heavily and contemplates what she wants to do. Anxiety makes her feel like her chest is a big black hole and she can't seem to make herself move. The scene of the dragonflies and Tristan's arrival had been distraction enough for her to put off the inevitable of checking out the situation again, but she can't keep fighting the urge to look no matter how much her anxiety is discouraging her.

Tristan takes a strand of her hair and wraps it around his finger a few times before he lets it fall back to her back. It holds a tightly curled shape momentarily before it straightens back out to a loose wave.

"Cali," he says barely above a whisper. "Whenever you're ready to go home, we can. It's up to you love."

Calandra turns and gives him a quick smile. "I have to go in there." She nudges her head towards the opening that she had explored and found the stranger through earlier. "I just have to get up the nerve to first." She says as she stares back into the distance.

"Ok, well I'm waiting right here with you." He says before he lies back onto the ground and leaves her alone with her thoughts.

"Thanks." She says but her voice sounds distant as she sees a flash of violet in her face and her anxiety turns to fear. She shakes her head to clear her vision again and sighs heavily as her thoughts return to her and the fear fades away.

****

Jarreth stares out the window of the bar lost in another world, her world. Should she have been able to affect him so much? He's done his fair share of traveling between the realms, never before with an actual purpose. It was usually always for selfish reasons, but it had never taken this much out of him before. He gulps down the dark purple liquid in the shot glass and raises it in the air as a signal to ask the bartender for another without actually turning to look at her.

The small framed woman glides over to him. Her hair is straight and blonde and hangs down to the middle of her thighs. She has a headband on to make sure that her hair doesn't cover the point at the tip of her ears. Only a few of the women still choose to show off their ears around here, Glyda just so happens to be one of them. She sways her hips as she comes towards him. The action gives the appearance that she is walking even though her feet are not actually touching the ground. Her wings are small enough that just looking at her from the front you can't tell she's flying. She's vain, as all pixies are, and always doing all she can to turn heads. It has much more effect on mortals than it does on other Fae of course, but that fact can't change her nature. Given that humans don't come to Faerie any longer, everyone has to do the best with what they have around here.

She brushes her hand along his as she takes the shot glass from him. "So, what'll it be this time Jare?" She bats her eyelashes flirtatiously at him as she speaks.

"Come off it already Glyda, and pour me a guilt." He says harshly.

She scoffs, but still brushes a finger lightly across his shoulders as she leaves to go make his drink. He rolls his eyes and goes back to his own thoughts. The emptiness inside him that has been plaguing him since he left Calandra's world doesn't seem to be getting any smaller despite the fact he's already had shots of luck, fear, and gluttony. It doesn't make any sense for him to be this empty after such a short experience. His thoughts are cloudy, nothing about the ordeal makes any sense. He was supposed to go there, entice her to come here through the ring, and leave. It was a clear-cut walk, he expected he would need one shot once he got back to refill. Going to the mortal world, even if it is only for a quick moment, takes a lot out of a faerie. Then again, usually those trips are meant for feeding off of the human and he didn't do that with Calandra. That must be the difference, he tells himself.

Glyda returns with his next shot, she

comes up beside him and makes sure to lean over and make a show of herself as she sets his shot down in front of him. Jarreth doesn't budge, and she walks away with another sigh of discouragement. Jarreth is the only one in the bar at this time of day. Everyone else is busy about other business for the day. When the bell above the door rings, he turns to see who it is and scoffs when Drake walks through.

Drake wears his normal mostly black attire and his dark hair is slicked back to make sure he can use his opaque violet eyes to his advantage when he comes across women. He glides in and turns directly towards Jarreth and heads to his table. He sits next to Jarreth without so much as looking at him.

"Glyda— the usual," he demands, "you know my taste dear." He adds a smirk to it before he turns back to Jarreth. "So, how did it go?"

Jarreth hasn't responded to or even acknowledged Drake's presence yet when Glyda returns to the table with Drake's order. The contraption looks like an old apothecary tool, it's silver and has designs engraved into the sides. It has a small burner at the bottom and a triangle shaped shot glass sits over it. She sets a brown glass jar with a thick liquid and a lighter next to it. She drapes her arm around Drake's shoulder and leans her body slightly against his.

"There you are sweets." She smiles down at him.

After he checks to be sure she brought everything he needs, he looks up at her with a daring smile. "Thanks love." He says and makes sure to flash his eyes at her.

Pixies don't blush, although if they could, she probably would have. Desire flashes through her eyes nonetheless. "Anything else I can do for you?" she asks.

"Not right now." He says and immediately withdraws his attention from her and turns to his things in front of him.

Jarreth gulps down his drink quickly and hands the glass to Glyda. "Lust," he says and motions for her to leave.

"Two in one visit?" Drake asks curiously.

"This will be five actually!" Glyda says before she slips away.

Jarreth rolls his eyes at her, not that she would care even if she had actually seen him do it. "It went fine Drake. It's done, and I'm sure that her interest is piqued." He looks at the things sitting in front of Drake. "So you're still on that stuff?" He asks in an attempt to change the subject.

"Always," Drake says simply.

Drake takes the bottle of liquid and fills the glass with the thick, dark red liquid. He lights the burner at the bottom. The flame is blue and then flashes purple. The liquid starts to bubble slightly and Drake quickly turns the burner off and blows on the liquid twice before he picks the glass up and gulps it down quickly. He leaves his head turned upwards and his eyes closed, holding it in his mouth to enjoy it thoroughly before he swallows. He then returns the glass back to the contraption and starts the motions over again.

"You should try it Jarreth, I promise you wouldn't regret it." He says as he fixes himself another.

Jarreth simply nods as Glyda brings his next shot over and leaves it on the table without saying a word to either of them.

"Still stuck on your small cups of sugar and spice and all that nonsense I see. Having a bit of trouble today since we're already up to five." Drake says as he takes his next shot. "Obviously you didn't do everything you should've while you were there or you wouldn't need five." Drake glares at him. "Or is it that this girl doesn't have any emotions?" Drake asks and he is suddenly intrigued.

"No, she definitely has them. I just didn't see a need in feeding off the girl. I calmed her at one point, but didn't take anything for my own use." Jarreth takes in his latest shot and concludes that the emptiness simply isn't going to be filled, though he's still unsure of why.

"Oh Jarreth, if you didn't have so many dang emotions, you just might be able to function properly," Drake says as he works on another shot. "I can lend you some of this if you'd like, it's much more substantial you know."

"I function just fine Drake. I did what I was supposed to, she should be here in the next day or so."

"*Should...* as in you're not sure? You didn't intrigue her enough because you didn't feed did you? Do I need to ensure that she gets here myself?" Drake asks and rage fills his voice.

"Look!" Jarreth says defensively as he holds up his shot glass once more. "We knew this would be complicated as she's already tied to a human. Her feelings there are deeper than we anticipated Drake. I did what I could, feeding wouldn't have changed anything. Her dad has been hiding everything from her though, so hopefully that will give her enough of a draw to come find out for herself."

Drake takes his shot as Glyda comes back for Jarreth's shot glass. "What now?" She asks.

"I don't care, anything." He says and the anger from the situation with Drake laces his words.

"Glyda you may take this, I am done."

Drake says as he runs his arm over hers. Glyda gladly takes the contraption and heads back over to the bar.

"I trust that you can entice her just fine Jarreth. I know what you are, even if you don't want to admit it. You're perfectly capable of doing what needs to be done no matter how tied she is to some human. Although I do believe I know a way to help her decide to come." Drake smiles mischievously.

"You know she has to come through the ring alone, without any assistance, that's the only way we'll know for sure." Jarreth rolls his eyes at Drake's usual smugness.

"I'm sure she will be marked upon her arrival or shortly after and we'll know one way or another. Either way, my plan doesn't consist of assisting in her entrance, just giving her more motivation to come." Drake smirks again.

"Leave her alone Drake!" Jarreth stands defensively in front of him.

"Oh I will Jarreth. Do your thing, and I'll leave her alone, just like I did Echo." Drake glares directly at Jarreth with that comment and his eyes flash black momentarily before they return to their normal opaque violet.

Glyda returns and puts a shot of bright pink liquid in front of Jarreth before she turns to Drake and leans into him. "Now what else can I get for you sir?" She asks and places a finger on his chin to make him look down at her.

"Yes I do believe I need one other thing, come to think of it." Drake smirks. "How about we get ourselves out of this bar dear? You don't mind, right Jare?" Drake looks back up at Jarreth as he wraps an arm around Glyda and pulls her closer to him.

Jarreth takes his shot and slams the glass back down on the table and it shatters. "No, do whatever you want Drake, I have my own matters to attend to." He says as he turns away.

"As do I." Drake calls after him before he leans down and starts to kiss Glyda. "One minute dear," he says as he pulls away. "How about you go get ready to leave and give me one moment to do something."

"Gladly!" She walks away, her hips sway even more than usual as she does.

Drake puts a hand on his temple. "Tristan." He says as he closes his eyes and mouths a few more words. A wicked smile comes over his face and he moves his hand back to his side and disappears behind the bar.

Chapter 7
Control

The conversation had taken many twists and turns. Calandra and Tristan had discussed her father, Tristan's parents, what they would do after high school, and even touched a bit on religion and beliefs. Calandra had a need for distraction, though she refuses to admit to herself that she may be procrastinating. There's something physically keeping her from searching for the answers, which means she can't really be to blame. Tristan was the one to start the conversation anyways. She was just taking it upon herself to be sure it doesn't end until she's ready. Plus it would be rude for her to ignore him. The vulnerability of being here, the fact she knows she needs to look for something that she isn't even sure she wants to exist or not, it all leaves her feeling raw and Tristan, as always, takes the edge off of that feeling.

    She rolls over to her side and faces Tristan. She places her head into his chest and clings tightly to him as he caresses her hair. The sun beats down on them and the soft buzz of the dragonflies still fills the air, which only intensifies Calandra's anxiety and her need for a distraction.

    Tristan doesn't believe any of the things that Calandra had explained she experienced earlier, he thinks it was another one of her daydreams and it seemed like more to her because she had been so emotional before it happened. Of course he would never actually tell her that he doesn't buy into the possibility of it being real though. Tristan isn't the kind of person to just squash down anyone's beliefs or feelings, even if he is completely sure they are wrong. He's a sensitive person, and always finds a round about way to get to the point, a way that keeps anyone from getting their feelings hurt. He had been nothing but a quiet support since she had explained her feelings about the experience to him.

Calandra breathes in Tristan's scent and wraps her arms around him tighter. All of a sudden, Tristan somewhat forcefully rolls over to be on top of her, pulls himself up, and veers over her. The shock of Tristan's sudden change in attentiveness sends a tinge of nervousness through Calandra. She looks up at him to question his motive. His eyes stare straight through her. They are their normal shade of baby blue, which usually intoxicates her, but there's something different about them now. They aren't as soft and knowing as they usually are, the safety they usually convey is gone. They are hollow as they stare down at her and his face is blank.

"Tristan?" She whispers as she reaches up and touches his cheek.

He doesn't respond in any way, he simply looks blankly at her. There are no emotions on his face at all.

"Tristan?" Calandra runs her hand up the side of his face and through his hair as she tries to steady her breathing.

Tristan slowly rolls off of her and sits straight up. He stares off into the trees now, in the direction she has been purposely avoiding. His face is still expressionless, his eyes are still not fully there. He doesn't seem to acknowledge that she's even here at all. He doesn't seem to be aware of anything at all, he's focused on something off in the distance. Calandra begins to wonder if he is even there at all. She has never seen him act like this before, like a zombie.

He slowly stands and takes longer than he should need to steady himself. He stands still, he doesn't even appear to be breathing, and he continues to stares at the spot. Calandra stands up next to him, unsure of what she can do to help him. She reaches out to take his hand, but before she makes contact, he walks off towards the woods.

"Tristan, seriously, what is going on? Where are you going?" she asks. A mixture of worry and frustration fills her as she follows after him.

He walks slower than usual and without his normal stance. He stands too straight and is carefully thinking through every movement he makes as if it is somehow forced. The dragonflies start to fly frantically around her and buzz louder than ever. One lands on her shoulder, Calandra gasps when she realizes it looks identical to the one that was here when she met Jarreth earlier. The dragonfly perches on her shoulder, angled towards her. She shakes her head to refocus and walks on to follow Tristan.

Her heartbeat grows faster and harder, she knows where he is going and everything looks all too familiar for comfort. She has to look behind her to see the creek, in the cloud of her thoughts that fill her as she frantically follows a zombie-like Tristan, she somehow has no recollection of walking through the creek, or getting here at all. She sees the vine wall and she doesn't need to walk through it to know what will be on the other side of it.

"Tristan, please just stop already!" she calls desperately after him to no avail.

Her breathing grows more unsteady when she sees Tristan disappear through the vines. She doesn't want to go through them. She isn't ready to see what lies behind it, to see that it is real. The thought of seeing that everything Jarreth told her is true brings the rawness back to her chest. She can't fathom a reason as to why Tristan has gone there or how he even knew where to go. She didn't tell him anything about the location of the spot other than the general direction. Yet somehow, he had purposely walked straight to it. She takes a deep breath, looks down at the dragonfly that is still perched ever so faithfully on her shoulder, pulls the vines aside, and walks through the opening.

The buzz from the friend on her shoulder

stops instantly, there's no noise at all. Everything seems so different and feels totally empty here without Jarreth, but it looks just the same. There's something about being here that sends a sudden peace through her. She looks around, and that peace and serenity disappears when she sees where Tristan is going. He's walking straight towards the ring of mushrooms and flowers, the ring that is the portal into Faerie.

"Tristan!" She yells louder than she means to and instantly realizes it feels wrong in the beauty of this place.

Calandra closes the gap between them and takes his arm to stop him, he turns on his heels to face her. There is no recognition, his eyes and face are still just as blank as they have been since the moment he stood up from the spot in her sanctuary. His cheeks appear to be sunken in.

"Just let him go." Tristan's mouth moves and his voice comes out, but the words aren't his.

"Him?! Him who Tristan? What is going on with you?" Calandra asks frantically.

Without another word, Tristan yanks his

arm from her and walks straight into the ring. The moment he crosses over the ring of flowers, he is suddenly back to himself. His eyes fill with warmth and brightness again, his face finally shows recognition. But those things quickly fade into fear and confusion.

"Cal! Cal!" He calls from the circle and tries to walk back towards her. Before he completes a full step, the glow that Calandra still wanted to believe was an odd reflection from the sun expands and lifts over him. With a flash, it is gone and so is Tristan.

Calandra screams and collapses onto the ground. The dragonfly still rests still on her shoulder. Jarreth's words go through her mind, no mortal is supposed to be able to go into Faerie without being accompanied by a faerie. So how had Tristan just crossed over?

"Was it because of me?" She asks, even though the dragonfly is her only company. "I didn't actually accompany him though. I was right here, unable to help him. He didn't even want to go...so why did he?" The dragonfly buzzes.

Calandra wonders if she had really expected some kind of a response out of it. Somehow the noise is enough to soothe her momentarily and allow her clouded mind to clear slightly. "I have to go get him." She tells the dragonfly. It takes her a moment to gain the confidence to do what she knows she has to. "If I'm really part Fae then I'll be able to go, the same way I somehow sent Tristan there."

The reality suddenly hits her hard, she feels it slam into her chest. Being part Fae is already causing problems and she only found out this morning through what she now wishes had actually been just a vivid daydream. Her thoughts start to flood through her and they mix with the questions that her subconscious tries to find answers for. The buzz on her shoulder reminds her that she isn't helping Tristan in any way by sitting here wasting time. She stands and takes a deep breath before she walks towards the ring.

Just before she crosses over the line of flowers, the dragonfly flies away. The glowing ring expands and lifts above her. Her head swims around and she suddenly sees a flash of lavender. Her feet leave the ground momentarily and she is falling into something. Her feet land on hard ground again, but it is still dark, or her mind is at least. She closes her eyes to try and focus herself. When she opens them again, she realizes she's in a field that looks almost identical to the one she just left, only this one is much larger. She focuses further and realizes the lavender flash she had seen was actually a set of eyes that are now coming towards her.

A tall, lanky man walks towards her, glides really more than walks. His every move seems like a piece of perfection. He wears mostly black clothes, black pants that are tighter than they probably need to be, a white shirt that is mostly hidden by the black trench coat that hangs over him. His hair matches his coat and lies messily around his face. His eyes stand out against all the dark that surrounds him, they are bright and match Jarreth's in opaqueness. But there a big difference between his eyes and Jarreth's. When Jarreth had looked at her, she felt some sort of peace and comfort. Looking at this man's eyes she feels an odd mixture of fear and temptation.

"Calandra." he says, his voice is deep and intimidating.

"Where is Tristan?" she asks. She is far too worried to care how he knows her name exactly.

"That's your first question my dear?" he asks nonchalantly.

"Yes of course." she replies simply.

He closes the gap between them faster than he should be able to. His eyes don't leave hers as he walks, he never falters in any way.

"Shouldn't your first question be about this?" He places his hand over her left shoulder and gently cups it, he slowly runs his hand across it. His touch sends chills through her, but not the good kind like Jarreth's had.

Calandra gasps once his hand is gone and she sees the dragonfly. It isn't a real dragonfly perched on her shoulder like she has been becoming somewhat accustomed to of late. This is a mark, some sort of a tattoo that has never been there before. It's stunning. It sits at an angle, its head faces towards her. Its wings are a breathtaking mixture of pinks and purples. On the left wing is a swirl of a beautiful baby blue through the center, and on the right wing, a matching swirl of lavender. Its eyes are a breathtaking shade of turquoise and it's body a bold shade of burgundy. It appears to be three dimensional as if there was actually a dragonfly perched on her shoulder looking at her, watching over her, much like the few dragonflies have done for her in her last few visits to the woods.

"What is it?" she asks, unable to take her eyes off of it.

Not only does it look like a tattoo that has been there forever, but also it seems as if it belongs on her shoulder. How had she randomly received a tattoo without knowing it? Without pain? Without healing? Was this somehow the effects of the trip here? The questions cloud her mind making it hard to focus on the task at hand.

"That, I am not willing to answer for you." he says and his smile turns quite wicked. "However, I am sure once Jarreth arrives he will fill you in on a few things, though not as many as he should I'm sure."

"Jarreth? Where am I? And who are you?" Calandra's head spins from all the questions that surge through her.

"You, dear, are in Faerie of course. That's what happens when someone of your— stature— steps into the ring. I, you will do well to remember, am Drake."

The memory of stepping into the ring flashes through her mind and reminds her once again what she was here for. Tristan is here somewhere, he has to be. She had accidentally sent him through to Faerie after he'd stepped into the ring.

"Where is Tristan?" she asks again. "And why did he come here?" She knows it wasn't of his own will. Something was controlling him, something made him come here. He couldn't have even possibly known where the ring was on his own, let alone known to use it to enter the world of Faerie. He had looked so frightened for the split second between him stepping into the ring and being taken to Faerie, the split second when he was actually there.

"He came here because I asked him to, and he is safe for now, that much you have my word on. I don't give my word to many, so you know." Drake's eyes remain on her shoulder as he speaks.

Was that supposed to be comforting? "Why would you ask him to come to Faerie. Better yet, why would he listen?" The fear is clear in her voice though she tries to keep it at bay, but everything is just bit too much for her to be able to control it.

"Drake—" Jarreth's voice comes from somewhere behind her.

Calandra turns around and sees that Jarreth looks identical to the way he had before, in the meeting that started all of this drama. Suddenly her fear and all of the emotions that have been welling up inside her disappear.

"Jare." Drake says with a laugh undertone. "I had just finished explaining to the girl that you would explain some things to her. She does seem to be a bit confused." He still stares at her shoulder.

Jarreth's hand touches her shoulder where the new mark is, and sends the oddest sensation through her body. His fingers trace along the body of the dragonfly before he traces down her arm and he drops his arm back to his side. His face is twisted into a mix of emotion, his eyes are somewhat sad, but there is also a trace of a smile.

"I told you." Drake says he finally takes his gaze from Calandra's shoulder and looks up at Jarreth.

Jarreth simply nods. "I'll take it from her Drake. You've done enough damage I'm sure." He says coldly.

Drake nods back. "As will you, I'm sure." He says before he turns on his heels and walks away from them.

Calandra still has no idea where Tristan is, but Drake apparently does. Her questions are still somewhere inside of her, but she can't seem to make herself ask them again. Sadness threatens to overtake her, and with less effort than usual, she's able to fight it down.

Jarreth places his arm around her back and hooks his hand against her right hip. He looks down at her shoulder once more.

"Come Calandra, I will take you to my house, and we will talk about everything I know you are dying to ask."

She doesn't ask questions, doesn't wonder what she should do, she simply sighs and lets him lead her.

Chapter 8
Questions

It strikes Calandra as slightly odd that the buildings of Faerie don't look much different from those of the mortal world. They walk through a town that is full of strips of different businesses; restaurants, bars, and stores. It's much more normal than Calandra had expected it to be. Although as she looks around, she realizes that the people and the landscape tell a very different story.

For one, the people of Faerie still appreciate nature. Even though they use the land to build the things they need to live a civilized life, they don't cut down every single bush, tree, and speck of grass to do so, like most of the mortal world seems to. A few of the buildings even have trees and plants that grow along the sides of them. Vines drape over the buildings like a blanket and cover the sides with intricate green labyrinths. The road is cobblestone and appears much more antique than the buildings that surround it. And beyond the buildings the grass, trees, and flowers are absolutely stunning.

The people are intriguing. Some seem normal, like Jarreth and Drake do, though none of them really dress normal if you're judging by the moral world, and none of them have normal eyes. All of their eyes are opaque and colors you would never see on a human. It's the one Fae trait that Calandra suddenly wishes she had inherited, beautiful Fae eyes. People had always told her that she had an amazing and unique eye color, tawny with random orange streaks throughout. Her eyes especially stand out against her pale white skin. Calandra swears some of their eyes flash different colors when they look at her as they pass. She can't quite decide how this should make her feel. She hasn't really felt much of anything since Jarreth's arrival, come to think of it.

Jarreth quietly walks beside her, his arm is still around her waist, and he gently guides her along. They haven't said anything since they left the field where Calandra entered into Faerie. Jarreth occasionally gives a greeting nod to people that pass, but he never says a word. Calandra bites her bottom lip and tries to work up the nerve to ask questions, or at least to say something.

"Why are they all staring at me?" She finally asks when she suddenly becomes aware that if the few Fae that walk past her without staring as they pass quickly turn around to stare after they have walked past her. Calandra swears that their eyes flash different colors as they watch her as well.

Jarreth pulls his other arm up and places his hand over the dragonfly on her shoulder and speeds up a bit.

"What does it mean?" She pries again.

Jarreth looks at her and turns his mouth up slightly into somewhat of a smile, and without a word, turns right back to looking at where they're going. Calandra sighs in aggravation. But as soon as the sound leaves her mouth, the emotion is gone. With some force, she finally stops walking and plants her feet firmly into the ground. Jarreth turns to face her, his arms don't move from her.

"What are you doing to me? Why don't I feel anything? I know that I should!" She tries to force frustration into her voice, but of course she can't make herself actually feel it.

Jarreth sighs and looks down at the ground in front of her. "Just trying to help. I'm not using them for myself, simply trying to make you more comfortable." He looks back at her once he finishes the far too unclear explanation.

"Is that supposed to tell me what you're doing? I need answers or something Jarreth, not riddles!" She removes his hand from her left shoulder, where the dragonfly mark now is. She steps away from him a bit so he's no longer touching her in any way and she is far enough she can't feel the spark radiating from him. She puts her hand on her hips, determined to at least attempt to look like she's feeling some sort of emotion even though Jarreth obviously knows she isn't and is the reason behind it.

Her attempt makes him laugh slightly. Calandra glares at him and becomes suddenly aware that everyone around them has stopped walking and is staring. Jarreth takes her left hand into his and brushes his thumb across her knuckles.

"Just let me take you somewhere we can be alone and I promise I'll tell you everything." His eyes plead with her as he says it.

The stares burn through her and she knows her self-conscience should be in overdrive. Defeated, she surrenders to his request. Not that she has a leg to stand on to fight against him really. She's in another world where she knows no one, her boyfriend has apparently been kidnapped, she has a random tattoo, and everyone is staring at her. What was she supposed to do exactly? The only thing she has that is familiar at all is Jarreth and somehow she doesn't think she can say no to him, even if she wanted to. She has come to the reasoning that she really has no other option but to do whatever he asks.

They finish the walk through town in silence. Calandra tries to ignore the stares and look like she belongs, though she is more than sure that her eyes and the mark on her shoulder are a dead giveaway that she doesn't. They veer away from the town down a small dirt road that turns into a small dirt path that winds through the most breathtaking woods Calandra has ever seen.

Birds, dragonflies, and small faeries fly all around. It should all be very peaceful and relaxing, and it is, until the thought crosses her mind that this could be very similar, if not identical, to how girls get kidnapped. For all practical purposes, walking with strange men though woods, in a world you know nothing about and where no one can save you is probably not one of the brightest ideas Calandra's ever had. The fear of course isn't felt. Somehow Jarreth is being sure of that. Calandra stops dead in her tracks and instantaneously Jarreth stops and turns to look at her.

"We're out of town and alone now so stop whatever you're doing! I want to feel it." she demands. Jarreth opens his mouth to protest, but his eyes look drained, and he gives in.

In an instant Calandra is overwhelmed, she begins to fall backwards and Jarreth reaches behind her to steady her. Fear, anxiety, confusion, longing, temptation, helplessness, they all turn into a black cloud that buries itself deep into her chest and stretches out to the pit of her stomach. She swallows hard and tries to regain herself again.

"Take it back!" she says breathlessly and shakes her head.

With a small smile, everything washes away

from her instantly. She audibly takes in a breath she didn't realize she had been holding in and focuses on trying to steady her breath. Jarreth's hand bares into her back harder as if he is preparing to keep her from falling back again.

"I'm okay." She assures him.

Jarreth pulls her towards him and leaves their bodies only a few centimeters apart. There is a strange heat radiating from him that she is ultimately aware as it seeps into her. He stares directly into her eyes and doesn't blink. Calandra is totally unsure of what it means or how to make it stop. He looks like he wants to say something, but is unable to do so.

Jarreth finally breaks the moment with words. "We're almost to my place, I'll explain everything when we get there." he says.

Calandra realizes that his eyes no longer look drained like they had earlier, they are back to the normal dazzling state that Calandra remembers from her dream and he looks refreshed somehow.

"Though if you wish to start the

questioning now, you may." He finishes and pulls his gaze from hers. He takes a sideways glance at her shoulder before he starts to walk again.

Unable to bring herself to question it, Calandra follows suit. Something about him pulls her in and she isn't sure how it makes any sense. She has never been the stupid fall right into a trap kind of person, but she suddenly wonders if she is crossing into that territory now. Despite what fears she knows should be coursing through her given the situation, she can't seem to fight Jarreth. There is a current that seems to pass between their bodies as they walk. It is an icy heat that makes her feel more alive than she ever has before. So she walks with him, even if it means she is walking straight to her death.

"What exactly is it you're doing to me?" She asks and the heat immediately rises into her cheeks. "My feelings, I mean, the emotions— how is it you can take them away exactly?"

"It's part of the type of Fae that I am. Different types of Fae have different— cultures, so to speak. We do different things, act different ways, have different morals." He leaves the rest of the explanation off and it hangs in the air.

"So, like a good and evil sort of thing or something?" Calandra realizes how stupid and immature the question is as soon as it spills off her lips, but she can't take it back now.

Jarreth stops at the question and turns to face her with a look of pain across his face. "It's not quite that simple when it comes to Fae Calandra, please remember that. There's not necessarily an easily defined line between good and evil, it's very blurred for anyone and even more so when it comes to Fae. We are creatures of desire, of temptation, and of pure emotions. What may be considered evil to mortals could just be run of the mill for our kind. Not even the good Fae, as you may like to think of them, are purely good. It isn't possible for a Fae to exist without some kind of evil in them, it's just who we are."

Calandra stares up at him and wonders if he is trying to give her some sort of warning about himself in a round about way. She decides to ignore it for the time being either way. "So, what are you doing with them then? You said earlier you weren't using them for yourself, just trying to help me. What does that mean exactly?"

Jarreth sighs and begins to walk again. "It means that normally I feed off of emotions. I don't allow myself to use emotions directly from humans anymore though. There are other ways to do it. I took your emotions from you, but I didn't use them to feed on. I simply took them to calm you down in an effort to help you out. I figured it was a lot to take in at once and it might be a bit too much for you."

Calandra remembers the stare off and how he suddenly looked less drained after it. Had he really not fed off of her emotions then? She pushes the thought away as a small house comes into view. It's more of a cottage really, a small brown wooden picket fence surrounds it. The house is made of a mixture of stone and wood with a brick walkway that leads to the glass front door. A pink tree that holds small flowers that look like firework explosions sits directly in front of the house. The grass is filled with blue and purple flowers that look like the flowers from the ring.

"Echo picked out that tree." He says as they walk along the little brick path.

The comment seems innocent enough, but it suddenly makes Calandra wonder how old Jarreth is exactly. She doesn't know what the morality rate of faeries is. *It's just who we are*, the statement from his explanation resonates through her mind suddenly. Was he including her in that statement as well?

"You said we." The thought doesn't make any sense as it escapes her lips.

He doesn't miss a single beat, Jarreth somehow knows what she means. "Yes Calandra, we. I told you before you are part Fae, it's how you were able to come here."

They walk into the house as Calandra tries to process what this all means. She is a faerie, at least partially. Maybe the warning he gave wasn't about him at all, maybe it was about her. But he can't possibly know anything about her, right? She sits down on the couch in the living room that the front door walks directly into.

"I'll be right back." Jarreth says as he walks into an entry way just off to the right.

Calandra looks around at the small but very open room. There is a large stone fireplace right in front of her and ivy wraps around it. The couch she sits on is blue and appears to be from another century, judging by the intricate wooden pieces along the arms and the back frame. There's a small wooden table in front of her and another off to the left side of the room that sits just under the only window. There's a very homey feel about the place. It comforts her probably more than it should. It smells of cedar and eucalyptus.

Jarreth returns with a silver tray that holds a blue teapot with a gold dragonfly, two matching teacups without handles, and a tall glass bottle with a bright pink liquid in it. He sets the tray on the table in front of her before he takes the seat next to her. He pours a glass of tea into the cup and sets it in front of her.

"Drink, it will make you feel better," he says, "I have sugar and milk as well if you'd like."

Calandra still stares at the glass bottle holding the pink liquid. It is thick and there are darker shades of pink swirling through it.

"What is that?" She asks without looking back to Jarreth as she says it.

"Like I said, there are other ways." He pours some of the substance into his tea and drinks it down immediately. "Now drink, please."

Calandra takes a small sip of the tea he poured for her. It's bittersweet, something floral mixes with a slight sour flavor that she can't quite place. It warms through her as she swallows it and surprisingly she does feel a little better. She takes another sip before she places the cup back on the table in front of her.

"What is this and what does it mean?" Calandra nods her head towards the dragonfly mark on her left shoulder. "It has to mean something since everyone seems so enthralled by it."

Jarreth pours himself another cup of tea topped off with the pink liquid and gulps it down before he starts in on his explanation.

"There was a time when Fae were allowed into the mortal realm and humans freely roamed in Faerie as well. Knowing about its existence that was all a mortal needed to be able to cross over. It was a time when the Fae and humans seemed to mix just fine, or as well as could be expected at least. There are things that some of our kind does, that doesn't necessarily sit right with all humans. My emotion feeding for instance, and there are other things for other types of Fae. We won't go into all the details just yet." A flash of something changes Jarreth's eyes to an eerie shade of gray before he continues. "Eventually, as it should have been expected to happen, one human crossed a line with the wrong faerie and things were sent into a bit of turmoil. To prevent an all out war between our worlds, we agreed to simply stay in our land and to ensure we did so, there were limitations placed on where we could go in the mortal world. In return, humans were prevented from coming to Faerie except under certain circumstances. A faerie must now accompany them over here and it must be for good reason. What we didn't expect upon doing this was that the absence of humans in our world would throw it off balance. Like I said before, there is no good and evil when it comes to Fae, and what we didn't fully realize at the time was that the human interaction was what helped to keep it all balanced. After a few failed attempts of a faerie taking over to reign and keeping order, the conclusion was made that no faerie was capable of doing so. We are incapable of having the right balance to properly keep order in our own land. But no human is capable of doing so either. For one, their lives are too limited and short and they don't have the power to be able to control Faerie." Jarreth pours himself another cup of tea and gulps it down.

Thoughts swirl through Calandra's mind as she watches him. No Fae can rule the land anymore, but obviously they are looking for someone to balance out their world again. Humans can't come to the world to be able to take over, and they wouldn't be able to rule either way. What Jarreth is saying and exactly how it involves her and the dragonfly on her shoulder suddenly clicks into place in her mind.

"So you need someone that is part Fae and part human?"

Jarreth stares straight through her with a sad look on his face.

"Yes." He says simply.

LAINY LANE

Chapter 9
Power & Temptation

The feeling like you've just had everything ripped straight from your body, that's the feeling that courses through Calandra. Her stomach clenches into a pretzel and her head swims in circles like a fish that's just been taken from the ocean and thrown into a small aquarium. How had her life become this exactly? She ponders the happenings of the last few days, the events that have flipped her world over completely. Like a globe that has been knocked off of a shelf and sent into a whirlwind fall, just waiting for the moment it will hit the floor and shatter into a million pieces.

"The good news is you'll get powers." Jarreth places a hand on her knee and she takes in the breath she's been holding since he said the word yes.

"Wait, just give me a minute please," she replies.

He has just sent her entire world spiraling around her and he wants to continue into his explanation like it was nothing. Apparently they expect the person destined to take over their world to have a stronger will or better control of their emotions than she does. She tries to wrap her brain around what he has told her. Surely this is all a crazy dream, she must still be caught up in one of her daydream experiences. Calandra wants more than anything to believe that this is all fake, that it's yet another one of her crazy daydreams and she'll soon find herself back in her car sitting on the side of the road while drivers speed past her. Yet something deep down inside of her won't let her believe its all imaginary. Somehow she knows that it's real, call it gut instinct or whatever you like, she just knows.

Suddenly the world isn't spinning anymore, instead it's thrown off of its axis somehow. Nothing makes sense anymore and a thick fog rolls into her head and clouds all of the thoughts going through it.

"Stop it!" She snaps at Jarreth.

Jarreth looks up at her perplexed. "What?"

"I want—" Calandra pauses, thinking carefully of how to choose her words before she continues. "I need to feel this."

"So feel it. What happened Calandra?"

So it's something else entirely now? Great, more things to make everything a bit more complicated. Calandra rolls her eyes and scoffs out of frustration.

"I swear I didn't do anything Calandra, please tell me what happened," Jarreth pleads.

"Clouds? Fog? Something...I don't know exactly, but my thoughts aren't there!" Calandra can't seem to make out a full sentence either apparently. She wonders if this is all stuff that she can blame on the mark that lies on her shoulder now or maybe the air of the new world she's in. She certainly doesn't feel anything like herself here.

Jarreth looks surprised as he picks up his glass once more and studies her.

"What?!" Calandra scoffs, she's becoming more than a little irritated.

"I assume it must be a vision. If you'd stop fighting it that is." Jarreth's voice sounds exasperated.

Calandra sighs. "Can things get just a bit more complicated please? I mean, really... I'm in another world as it is. Shouldn't I get a break from the drama? I thought that was how fantasy worked!"

Jarreth frowns over at her. "Unfortunately, yes they can, and not only that—" He breaks off and brushes his finger along the side of her face.

There's that cool burning sensation again. "They will," he finishes and looks back to his cup immediately.

Calandra sighs, falls back into the couch dramatically, and closes her eyes. Who would have thought her life could change so quickly in one day. She was a normal teenage girl just the other day wasn't she? One that had an overbearing father, oddly colored streaked hair, and more than unique eyes; but other than that, she was normal enough. A simple teenage girl with a quarterback boyfriend that no one quite understood how she managed to get. She had normal high school drama and she was an average height, slender girl with a slightly less than fashionable wardrobe.

Normalcy was something she has apparently been taking for granted all this time. Now she is being faced with an intimidating destiny and way too much new information. Her world is spinning out of control rapidly and she's just waiting for the moment when she finally flies off of it into oblivion. Which might actually be a welcome option right about now. Calandra sits against the couch and tries to focus on her breathing, to steady herself and make some kind of sense of things. She feels it start to open up inside her, the black hole that threatens her sanity all too often for her liking. The anxiety takes over all her efforts to calm herself. Her breathing starts to pick up and her heart begins to race.

"That—" she says without opening her eyes, "you may freely take, and I don't care what you do with it either."

Instantaneously, the anxiety melts away and Calandra relaxes into the slight comfort she gains from its absence. Her mind is still covered in a dense gray fog. The icy hot feeling slides up her arm slowly and is traced by a tingle that spreads throughout her entire body. She doesn't have to open her eyes to know that Jarreth is touching her. The sensation trails up her arm and slowly across her shoulder and stills there. The electricity slowly traces circles around where the new mark is on her shoulder. The current that his touch causes courses through her limbs and dissipates everything else. Her breathing slows, probably more than it should. The moments stretch out into something uncountable. A sense of belonging washes over Calandra.

Just as she finds herself feeling completely at ease and relaxing completely for the first time in a very long time, she hears water dripping and it causes an echo. It is a hollow sound that cannot be coming from inside of a house. The smell of dirt and copper fills her nose. A soft babble comes into focus. The gray fog slowly evaporates and a cavern appears in its place. The true beauty of nature lies in this most unlikely place. Stalactites and stalagmites make a maze of Mother Nature's finest artwork. The small light that comes through the opening of the cavern makes reflections of pinks, lavenders, and light blues off the face of the water and parts of the rocks surrounding her. The entire scene is breathtaking.

"Calandra." Tristan's voice brings her out of her state of amazement.

Calandra spins on her feet and finds he is

huddled in a corner. His face is dirty and his features are darkened from lack of sleep. There are tear tracks through the dirt on his face and his eyes are bloodshot.

"Wouldn't you be a sight for sore eyes if you weren't so different." His voice is cold and cruel, which is not normal for him.

Calandra tries to place his newfound coldness. He must be mad that she brought him here. She can't be that different, other than the dragonfly on her shoulder. She looks over and finds that it is indeed still there, proudly reminding her of her destiny that still lies ahead of her.

"Are you ok?" She asks as she walks over to him.

His arms are behind his back as if they are chained to the wall but Calandra doesn't see anything binding them. Bewildered, she goes to reach for them to try and pull them around and free him from his invisible captivity. Her hands tremble as they approach him but just before she touches his filthy arm with her fingers, the entire scene disappears into gray fog once more.

Calandra sits up with a gasp. Her eyes open wide and ferociously. She is still in Jarreth's house, he sits next to her and looks completely perplexed. His hand still rests on her shoulder.

"What was it?" Jarreth asks.

"I saw Tristan, I saw where he's keeping him." she says out of breath.

Calandra remembers the calm and the feeling that went through her at his touch and her nerves shoot up tenfold. "You did that didn't you? You made that happen? Was It even real at all?" She says it louder than she means to.

"No Cal, you relaxed and you quit fighting the vision. Please tell me what you saw. There is so much you do not know of visions, you can't understand what it means." He pleads and places his arms tentatively at his side.

"No!" She gets up off the couch with haste. "You are done explaining anything."

Without another thought Calandra bolts out the door. Her feet carry her faster than she ever remembers them being able to before. Her tears stream hot down her face and drip off her cheeks. She runs back the way she came, to the only place in this world she knows, back to where she entered into this world and as far away from Jarreth and the dark cloud he's just opened up on her world as she can possibly get.

****

The room is covered in dark paint. There is a small table next to the bed. One small lamp is the only source of light in the tiny room. The door is directly in front of him and there is a light coming in through the crack. Tristan sits on the bed, the cool air drapes over him like a heavy cloak.

Drake walks into the room, the same cool smile Tristan saw as soon as Calandra disappeared from his sight. Then he was sent here, to this small room, he has no idea where he is.

"Still alive?" Drake chuckles.

Tristan nods slightly.

"Here," Drake slides a tray with a sandwich and a water bottle onto the bed. "Eat up and enjoy," he says before he disappears back out the door and leaves Tristan to the dark closet of a room once more.

LAINY LANE

Chapter 10
Field of Innocence

The tree sits majestically at the edge of the field. It is the sister tree of the one in the almost identical field in the mortal world. Calandra still isn't exactly sure what that means, but she certainly doesn't remember the tree at home looking quite so— wise. This tree is tall and wide, showing that it's seen a lot in it's lifetime. There's trial there, about halfway up, the tree starts to tilt a bit. It's as if the weight of the world sat on it all of a sudden, and weighed it down from its true goal of growing straight up to the sun. But it won in the end, it still grew taller and taller, albeit tilted a bit. The beauty of the story in that one detail intrigues Calandra.

She walks over to the majestic tree and places her hand on the trunk gently. She can feel the pain radiating from it, the strength, and the will to continue on. This tree has prospered against all odds, even when it wasn't meant to. It comforts Calandra to see the possibility of it. A calming sensation runs through her. It comes straight from the tree, into her hand, and courses throughout her entire body. Belonging, purpose, and reason wash through her and she relishes in it, she soaks it all in. A new sensation renews her as the wind picks up around her. Her hair flies into the air and lightly blows in the breeze.

This isn't simply an emotion trying to communicate with her. This is destiny. The purpose of everything she's ever been through and is going to go through all lead up to this perfect moment. Calandra can sense the reality of it as she stands here touching the tree. This is what she must face, the road she must take even if she doesn't want to. The road less traveled on, she thinks. People always want to take the easy road. But not everyone has a choice, some must take the long rocky road and hope that it leads them somewhere beautiful at the end. This is Calandra's mission, and nature is letting her know in this moment.

The wind disappears in an instant and the rush of emotions leaves her skin at the exact same time. The earth is quiet again, calm. Calandra opens her eyes, though she hadn't realized she had closed them. Jarreth stands a few feet from her and he looks at her with amazement. Heat rises to her cheeks and she drops her hand from the tree and sits on the ground and rests her back against the tree, not wanting to break contact with it just yet. Jarreth's expression doesn't falter, he simply stands there as he waits for permission to approach.

"Come," she says and brushes the word off her hand at him. "You look kinda stalker-ish standing there staring at me like that, it's creepy." Calandra means it to be sarcastic but she sees a flash of pain cross his face as his eyes change to a dark cobalt blue for a moment.

Calandra feels like her head is in an aquarium. Too many thoughts will create a migraine pressure in your head. A fog settles in so that nothing is clear at all. How to figure out what's right and what's wrong is unfortunately something that has to be learned the hard way. No one can tell you and even if they could, if you're simply following the rules because it's what you're supposed to do, then you are missing the point.

Calandra has no idea who to trust and her heart races at the thought that Jarreth may actually be an enemy. Somehow his eyes tell her something different. There's something innocent about them, the opaqueness of them, the tranquility of the color of them, the softness deep within them. The way he can stare straight into you with them. Surely something so beautiful can't be evil, at least not completely.

"Would you like to know why you feel drawn to this place?" Jarreth asks.

"Who said I felt drawn to it?" Calandra doesn't mean for it to come out sounding as offensive as it does.

"You think it was simply coincidence that you came here when you needed a place to sort through things?"

"It's the only place that I knew because this is where I came through— right?" She asks, feeling suddenly unsure of something she had been absolutely positive about just moments ago.

"It is where you came to enter our world," Jarreth begins, "that, however, is not the reason your body led you here. This, Calandra, is the field of innocence."

"No, the place in my— whatever, was the field of innocence." Calandra corrects him as she remembers him saying the same line in the experience that started this whole ordeal.

"Yes and no," Jarreth replies simply.

"Your riddles really get old and irritating, is that like a Faerie thing or just a Jarreth thing?" Calandra scoffs.

"It's like a make you think and figure things out for yourself thing." Jarreth nudges her in the shoulder and flashes the most genuine smile Calandra has ever seen.

"Well, I've kind of had a long day, so how about you just give me this one?" Calandra hides her blush as best she can.

Jarreth laughs, "you are correct. Where we were in the mortal world is the field of innocence as well, they aren't exactly one in the same although they are connected. The one you are in currently has the full magic of Fae in it. Which is what you were experiencing when I got here."

Calandra goes back in her head to when she first encountered Jarreth and where she first learned of her faerie heritage. *You're back to the innocence of a child, ridden of all the untruths your people have made up over the years, and free to see what really is.* "The innocence of a child." Calandra mumbles without meaning to say anything.

"Yes Cal, the innocence of a child. The ability to know the truth, to believe what is real not because of probability or logic, but because you just know." Jarreth explains.

"So— like faith?" Calandra asks.

"I guess you could say that. However, faith isn't exactly something that is believed very widely here in Faerie."

Calandra stares blankly at Jarreth with the question written plain as day on her face.

"We tend to think that hope and faith are things humans invented to feel better about themselves. Kind of a way to make bad situations seem better because they think that something larger, more powerful, and more capable is in control and can make everything better. The way I see it, the only one who can control anything about your life is you. You're in control of what you become and what you do, the only thing that can make anything any better are your choices and how you decide to handle the situations that you are dealt."

Calandra takes a deep breath and looks down at the dragonfly on her shoulder with a slight frown.

"What is it?" Jarreth asks.

"I kinda thought this— was a symbol of hope," she says without taking her eyes off of the mark.

"Not hope Cal, support. That is the mark of destiny and it is a reminder that you have people behind you to help you achieve it. The field is also a reminder Calandra, a place you can come and know again what is right and wrong. A place to clear your thoughts and figure things out when nothing out there," Jarreth points away from the field as he speaks, "makes any sense and you can't tell what's up or down anymore. And trust me, if today wasn't enough of a sign, that is going to happen dear."

Calandra stares at him as she tries to take it all in. The way things have changed in just a few short days. Something should fill her; doubts, fear, nerves, but as she sits here and stares at Jarreth she feels none of those things. His eyes somehow manage to take it all away and bring her back to a state of serenity. The world, crazy as it is at the moment, disappears and feels just right.

"So, I take it if you don't believe in faith and hope there's not exactly any kind of a deity here either?" Calandra doesn't quite understand why that is the first thought that crosses her mind at the moment, but it is out of her mouth before she can stop it.

Jarreth chuckles, "no dear, faeries tend to believe in nothing but power. Magic and temptation is our controller. Trust me, if there were some kind of a deity out there, I highly doubt they would take too kindly to our kind anyway. We aren't exactly the most redeemable creatures, so to speak."

"I don't believe that," Calandra's hand rests on the soft grass slightly out to her side and she leans into it to support herself. She absorbs every word he says like a sponge, lingers on his every statement. She links them all together and tries to build a picture of what this world is like. The small piece that she has seen was a little more than troublesome in her state of mind at the time. Not to mention that she was only slightly intimidated by the fact that every single person was staring at her, or technically at her mark.

"What exactly don't you believe?"

"That you aren't redeemable. Everyone is supposed to be right? I mean if God made the world and everything in it, then surely he'd provide a way for everything to be redeemed, right?" Calandra isn't exactly the right person to be discussing the technicalities of something such as religion as she is filled with a million questions of her own regarding it. "So—" She begins a game of twenty questions in an effort to change the subject since she feels incapable of discussing the subject at hand, despite being the one that got them on the subject in the first place. "I take it from the stares I got on the way to your house everyone here knows what this means exactly." Calandra noses her face towards the dragonfly to indicate what she is referring to. It feels like a childish move to make, but she isn't sure what word to use to refer to it exactly.

"Your mark?" Jarreth seems to know all of her questions before she voices them. "There is only one thing it could mean Cal, and yes, that is why everyone was staring. There will be quite a stir over the next while about you." His smile beams into her and leaves her feeling suddenly exposed.

"Oh," she replies simply.

"That wasn't meant as an insult you know." Jarreth places his hand over hers. Heat spreads throughout her body and is followed by a cold tingling sensation. It relaxes her and eases up the tension that has been building in her head all day, she relishes in the feeling and lets it wash over her. "Calandra, there is a bit more that you must understand about what lies ahead for you here." His eyes flash a soft shade of midnight blue before they return to their normal shade of baby blue.

Calandra tries to ready herself for whatever is to come. "Do I want to hear or understand it?" She asks, "I am in a bit of an overload as it is."

"I know my dear, but you must hear it and

truly understand it as so many rely on you now." He leans his hand into hers and sends the surge of electricity and fire and ice back through her once more. His eyes look sad and Calandra's nerves build inside her like a brick wall despite the sensation that pools in her skin from Jarreth's touch.

Calandra takes in a cleansing breath and closes her eyes momentarily. "Fine, go for it," she sighs.

"Faeries are born out of imagination. People dreamt us up long ago. That's one of the reasons there are so many different types. Now there are many more types due to all of the mixing of blood that's been done over the years. But that's where evil comes from as well, it is created." Jarreth lifts his hand from hers and places it on her shoulder and rests it on her mark. "The mind is a much more powerful thing than humans could ever comprehend. Much too powerful for anyone to be trusted with. And it's even worse when they don't know the capabilities of it. But you, Calandra, must not only understand that but learn to control it as well. The power of your mind combined with the limited Fae powers and emotions you were given could make or break the entire universe. You have the power to destroy both of our worlds without even meaning to." He stares into her once more as he finishes his explanation.

The weight of the world, of two worlds, rests on her shoulders. She painfully pulls her gaze from Jarreth's and focuses on the tree. She wonders to herself what it was that made the tree bend and tilt the way that it does. What burden was placed on it? More importantly, how did it manage to hold the weight enough to still grow tall and strong, albeit just a little crooked? She wonders where that strength comes from and how she can get some of it for herself. The breeze picks up again and wraps around her body, it caresses her skin with a soft gentle whisper. Her hair picks up and dances in the wind, her skin tingles with a knowing sensation. Jarreth stares at her with the same sense of amazement as he did when he first saw her in the field earlier.

At that moment, she comes to the conclusion that whatever it is she must face, she can somehow manage it. No one knows their future or how to handle the situations that they are faced with, why should she be any different? Just because she now knows she has a big destiny in front of her? She is still the only one in control of how she deals with her life. The breeze leaves as quickly as it came and a chill rushes over her in its absence.

"That, my dear, is nature telling you that you can indeed handle it," Jarreth smiles knowingly.

Calandra smiles, and for once, it reaches her eyes. For once, she feels like she knows where she belongs and what she is meant for. Her heart seems to dance inside of her at the final sense of knowing she's right where she needs to be. She leans into Jarreth's hand and let's all of the emotions wrap tightly around her as she closes her eyes. Calandra sighs and lies in the soft grass beneath her. She lets the sun wash over her skin as she closes her eyes and finally relaxes.

"One more thing," Jarreth breaks her from the silence.

Calandra opens her eyes and gazes at him skeptically. "Do I even want to know?" she groans.

"Actually, this one I believe you do." He smiles, "I have a little something to show you." He stands up in one quick and fluid moment and reaches his hand out for her. "Come," he says simply and without any further questions, Calandra obliges.

LAINY LANE

Chapter 11
Gifted

As they walk through the woods, Calandra is starting to wonder what she should expect. She feels as if they've been walking forever and the woods seem to be growing denser the further they go in. "Where are we going exactly?" Calandra finally asks, unable to keep quiet any longer.

"You'll see," he smiles.

"Jarreth!" she whines.

Jarreth shakes his head. "Sorry, but that's not gonna work dear," he chuckles.

Calandra sticks her bottom lip out as far as she can. But Jarreth only looks at her for a moment before he turns back to the path ahead of them. "What about a hint?" She whispers.

Jarreth's smile widens and he leans in to her ear. "No need, we're here." He whispers and stops walking.

Calandra looks around, and is suddenly more confused than ever. The woods are still dense around them. There are lilies surrounding three of the trees just in front of where they stand and ivy runs down them. The ivy creates a wall in between all of the trees. "So— it's a tree?" Calandra spaces the words out.

Jarreth chuckles, "Technically speaking, yes." He steps in between two of the trees in front of them and brushes the ivy to the side. He holds his hand out inviting her to step in between the trees. Calandra looks at him skeptically. "Have I ever led you astray?" he asks.

"I'm not sure I can answer that just yet." She arches an eyebrow at him. After taking a moment to think, she sighs and accepts that even if he had, she would probably still do anything he asked her to do, so it's really a moot point.

To say she was breathless would be an understatement. There is a clearing through the trees that Jarreth sends her through. One tree stands in the middle of the clearing and it reminds her of the large tree in the field of innocence. The trunk of this tree is larger than any she's ever seen before. The tree itself is much larger than she imagined possible as well. The top of the tree is so dense you can't see through any of the leaves to see its branches. It is a beautiful sight of nature.

"The leaves never fall off." Jarreth is right behind her which startles her slightly. "They turn colors in the fall, but they will never fall off."

"Why?"

"To hide what's behind them," he explains.

She looks at him puzzled. Jarreth points to

the base of the tree trunk and Calandra suddenly notices something that she hadn't before. "Is that—" She walks over to the tree trunk and places a hand on it. "A door?" She traces the space that separates the door from the rest of the trunk.

"It was your mothers."

"My mothers? She lived here?" Calandra places her hand over the stub in the tree that is the doorknob, but she doesn't open it. Her brain suddenly seems to have quit telling her body how to move.

"Not for long, but yes. She lived here for a time. She didn't want to live anywhere in town though, she had a special affinity for nature, so naturally, this is where she wanted to be." Jarreth places his hands over her shoulders and nudges her towards the tree. "I'll let you go in alone for a bit."

Calandra takes a deep breath and finally turns the knob. The trunk is hollowed out and there is a set of spiral stairs that lead into the area in the tree branches. It is done in such a way so that the natural beauty of the tree is still in tact as much as it possibly can be. What was carved out to make the area for the stairs was also used to make the stairs themselves so that nothing was actually taken from the tree. Calandra slides her hand up the inside wall of the tree trunk as she walks up the stairs. It is rough, the indents and grooves of the tree show through, still left in its natural space.

The stairs step out into the living space. It is round and covers the entire circumference of the top of the tree. The entire place is made of wood. It is glossed over but still natural looking. The living room, kitchen, and dining room are all one big open area.

The living room is small and holds nothing but a small blue couch, a coffee table, and a large wooden hutch across from it. The table looks almost identical to the one in Jarreth's cabin. The hutch has ivy engraved into the edges of it. There is a small rug under the coffee table that is a beautiful labyrinth of blues, purples, and pinks. Windows line the entire area to create a beautiful mixture of leaves and ambient light. Calandra finds herself wondering how amazing it must look when the leaves turn colors for fall as Jarreth said they do. There are small slits in the wood above the windows to allow nature to come into the house as it pleases.

The kitchen is small and cozy. Everything is made of wood. There is a small row of cabinets against the back wall and one small sink. Across from it is a bar area with small wooden stools without backs. There are still dishes in the sink and a few appliances scatter the countertop. The dining room holds nothing but a small wooden table with two matching chairs on either side of it.

There is a sweet simplicity to everything, yet at the same time it's very elegant. It seems as though it was abandoned. Things are still things just lying around like the leave was unexpected. Calandra finds herself wondering about her mothers last day here. Standing in this place, the home that her mother had stayed in, Calandra feels more connected with her mother than she ever has before. It brings a peace to her that she has never felt. A comfort, a knowing that she is right where she is supposed to be. She has finally found herself. Her path ahead may not be easy, but life isn't supposed to be easy, regardless of what world it takes place in.

She didn't hear Jarreth coming up the stairs. He was in front of her wiping away a tear she that hadn't noticed was falling.

"Sorry." She says immediately and the heat rises to her cheeks.

"Never apologize for tears Cal, they are not a sign of weakness, but a sign of healing and of growth." Jarreth smiles reassuringly. "So, do you like it?"

Calandra sniffles up the remaining tears that threaten to break through and smiles. "Of course."

"Have you been upstairs yet?"

Calandra looks around. "I thought I was upstairs?"

"So, did you think she didn't have a bedroom anywhere?" He chuckles.

Calandra shrugs, "I guess I hadn't really thought much about it, I was too distracted."

Jarreth reaches out to her and Calandra places her hand in his. He walks her to the edge of the house in between the kitchen and the dining room. What Calandra had thought was a tall wooden cabinet turns out to contain another small staircase on the other side. The stairs are rather steep and narrow, but luckily there aren't too many of them as Calandra begins to feel her legs burning as they climb up them.

It is the coziest bedroom Calandra has ever seen and she automatically never wants to leave. The walls and floors are glossed over wood just like the downstairs. There is a wooden four-poster bed with a blue and purple quilt. There is a wooden trunk at the foot of the bed and two small end tables on either side of it. Each end table holds a small lamp with shades that reflect shadows of birds and sprites onto the walls. On the opposite side of the room is an armoire and next to it a small door that opens into a tiny bathroom.

"Why did you bring me here exactly?" Calandra turns to Jarreth who is still standing at the entrance to the room.

"Because it's yours now. Besides, I figured you might want a place to sleep. A place you'd feel comfortable staying."

Calandra smiles softly. "Thank you."

Jarreth smiles, but it doesn't look totally sincere, it looks somewhat sad. "I figured it might help you sort through things."

"Jarreth, I don't think where I live is going to help me sort through any of this."

"What would?"

"I don't know." Calandra looks around and sighs, still feeling a bit lost. "I mean, this does help. I can feel her here, I've never felt her before, not really."

"You really should trust in yourself a little more." He whispers as he takes a seat on the bed and motions for her to join him.

She tries to say something back, but it gets stuck somewhere between her throat and her mouth.

"You are an amazing person. If you weren't, you wouldn't be worth all the trouble you're causing." He smiles down at her.

"And here I thought you were trying to actually be nice!" She rolls her eyes.

"Not the most redeemable person, remember?" He winks.

"I already told you I didn't believe that!" She counters.

"So tell me Calandra, what is it you believe then?"

Calandra shrugs her shoulders. "I don't guess I've really figured that out just yet."

"You're still young, you have time to decide still," he smiles.

"Do I? How does anyone really know how much time they have? If you don't figure out the right thing to believe in before it's too late, I hear it can have some pretty dire consequences of the eternal sort."

Jarreth chuckles.

"Why is that funny?"

"I guess, being a faerie, I have a much different stance on eternal things." He stands up and walks to the doorway and begins walking downstairs without explaining anything further.

"Where are you going?" She calls down to him.

"To make some tea, no one can discuss anything of the eternal sort without a cup of tea."

"Where exactly is that rule written?" She runs down the stairs after him.

"If it isn't written somewhere, then someone should really write it down somewhere."

Calandra laughs. "What in like the tea instruction booklet?"

"Don't laugh Calandra, there are things in the world, regardless of the realm, that nothing other than a glass of tea can fix!"

"Yeah ok..." She takes a seat at the bar and watches him. "So where do you think Tristan is?" It occurs to Calandra that she has just wasted an entire day without looking for him at all and guilt washes over her.

"That is something we'll have to coax out of Drake I suppose."

"What's the deal with him exactly?" Calandra asks. Her short meeting with him had been anything but comforting or informative.

"He's— well, he's Drake."

"Yeah, that's real clear, thanks for that!" She rolls her eyes as Jarreth places a teapot identical to the one from his house in front of her and pours her a cup.

"Remember what I said about figuring things out for yourself?"

Calandra groans. "Any chance this is one of those things that tea will fix?"

"There's only one way to find out!" He laughs.

Chapter 12
Captive

Time drags on in slow lulls. Each breath becomes an act of force. Thoughts come and go at random intervals. Hours, minutes, days; they all blur together into an unfathomable jumbled mess. Possibilities, thoughts, and escape plans all ramble through his head constantly somehow tied together like an endless dream that continuously changes scenes. The music and laughter outside of the closet room doesn't make anything any easier. There is a constant flow of trays filled with mediocre food brought into the room with a crude joke or comment and then it's back to black. Alone and helpless doesn't begin to describe the predicament that Tristan finds himself in.

The entire place has been quiet for what seems like hours. Sleep has only come in completely random fits for his entire stay here. When all you have is a dark room to sit in, sleep is really the only form of entertainment you have. At least in his sleep, he can find Calandra and feel happy and safe again. Dreams are the only place that the haunting thoughts of where Calandra may be actually leave him alone and he's free to hope for the best. When he's awake, the fear that Calandra is being held captive somewhere as well makes him nauseous. Drake hasn't been any help with information despite Tristan's best efforts to get details out of him, which only makes Tristan's imagination take the possibilities to a whole new level of paranoia.

There is no separation of time in a situation such as this. Everything is one blurred mess without meaning. It takes what seems like hours, but could in actuality only be a matter of minutes, for Tristan to convince himself to go and explore in the absence of noise. He lingers with his hand on the doorknob, and takes a few moments to convince himself that he has the nerve to open the door and leave. There haven't actually been any orders to say he has to stay in this hole he's in. It was something that he just assumed. Technically speaking, he can't break any rules if none have been placed upon him in the first place. With that final convincing thought, he turns the knob and slowly opens the door without the slightest idea of what to expect to see on the other side.

The door he walks out of is in the middle of a hallway. Tristan looks to the left and sees no more doors, there is nothing but darkness. *Odd,* he thinks. What's the point of a hallway that goes nowhere exactly? Deep down, something tells him he should ignore it and turn to the right. He lingers in the doorway and attempts to fight back the curiosity that tempts him to go to the left anyways. After a few moments that feel like an eternity, he gives in and turns to the left anyways. The darkness takes over him and feeds into his nerves, it courses through his veins and heightens every sense in his body.

    Tristan reaches the end of the hallway and feels around the seeming dead-end wall in front of him. About halfway down he realizes it isn't just a wall after all. He can feel the start of a frame, a doorframe, and a very small door. He also feels some sort of intricate woodworking in the frame, he traces along the notches in the wood as he tries to make out some sort of pattern. Finally he distracts himself from the detail and kneels down and starts to feel around for a doorknob. He sighs in frustration when he realizes he can't seem to find one. Well the hallway turns and leads to this, so it has to be more than just some decoration, surely it opens somehow. Tristan frantically continues to run his hand along the wood searching for anything to indicate a way to open the small entry. Just as he feels a small notch and starts to inspect it and figure out how he can use it to make it come open, his heart drops into his stomach.

Ahem. He hears the noise at the same time that he realizes there is a flicker of light behind him.

"Crap!" He murmurs as he stands and turns to face his kidnapper.

Drake is tall and slender, dark shadows seem to always follow him and frame his face. His eyes are an odd opaque lavender color and he has about as much patience as a cat while it waits on a mouse to come out of it's hole and walk straight to its impending death. This isn't going to end well.

"You know Tristan," his voice is cold, "leaving your room is one thing. But trying to wonder through something that is obviously a secret compartment is quite another."

Tristan stands with his mouth hanging open, unsure of what move he's supposed to make. He is cornered against the end of the hallway after all, it's not like there's really much he can do really.

"Come," Drake says and motions his arm towards Tristan.

Tristan takes a gulp and breathes in finally. Without a choice, he walks to the other end of the hall and follows Drake through to the rest of the house. Drake leads him into the living room. There isn't much light throughout the house, there are only a few scarce windows scattered here and there and dark curtains cover them to keep most of the sunlight out. The furniture is all-dark and appears to be from another century. There is one couch and a small black table in the living room. Tristan notices another piece of furniture at the other end of the room, an armoire with a few frames on top, but they are too far away to make out anything about them.

"Sit," Drake says cooly and walks out of the room.

Tristan's heart beats rapidly. His thoughts are speeding like a freight train. Suddenly he wishes that he had just stayed in his little closet room. He really didn't think anyone was home, surely at times the house has to be empty. A few minutes later, a girl walks through the room. She is tall but petite with long blonde hair and small wings protruding from her shoulder blades. Tristan shakes his head as she walks out the front door and slams it behind her. Too much time in a tiny dark room must be playing tricks with his head. Drake returns to the room seconds after the woman leaves with a teacup in his hand. He places it on the table in front of Tristan.

"Drink," he says simply as he takes the seat beside Tristan. Drake turns to face Tristan on the couch, he places one leg up on the couch and lays it across his other knee. He stares blankly at Tristan as he waits for him to obey.

Tristan looks at the cup, unsure of what to do. Taking strange drinks from the person that has been keeping you locked in a closet more than likely isn't exactly the brightest of ideas. Although Drake has been feeding him and nothing bad has happened to him as of yet, other than the boredom of being in a dark room for who knows how many days now. If he meant him harm, surely he would've acted on it by now.

"It's tea Tristan, now drink. Trust me if I wanted you dead, you would be. Rest assure that I wouldn't be kind enough to make it as simple as drinking something either." Drake says it as if it should be reassuring somehow.

"What good am I to you anyways?" Tristan asks as he takes the cup and lets the warm liquid warm his chills.

"Honestly, not much anymore."

The chills return tenfold. "So you don't— need me?" Tristan's voice shows his fear.

"Don't flatter yourself Tristan. You were bait and you've served your purpose already." Drake flicks his hand in the air to reiterate his point.

Tristan continues to sip on his tea and tries to piece the puzzle together and make sense of this information. Bait. Bait for what? He takes a sharp intake of breath and chokes on his tea as he realizes the only thing he could be bait for. Calandra. Her name rings through his mind and brings a rush of emotions with it.

"By the look on your face, I'm assuming you've finally figured it out," Drake says with a ghost of a smile. "I wasn't sure Jarreth did his job right, so I needed bait to be sure that Calandra came." Drake points at Tristan as he says the last part.

"Her daydream?" Images suddenly start to run through his head as he pieces more things together and he attempts to decode everything Drake is saying.

Drake nods to let Tristan know he's on the right track.

"And here is where exactly?" Tristan hasn't been able to ask any questions since he's been here and he plans to take full advantage of the opportunity while he still can.

"Faerie." Drake says simply as if it should have been obvious.

Tristan's jaw drops.

"You didn't put that together when you saw a faerie walk out of my house? Surely Calandra mentioned that's what Jarreth said she was... at least partially." Drake's eyes flash black before they return to lavender and a mischievous smile crosses his face.

Of course Calandra had mentioned that, Tristan had also known that she must have been entirely too stressed and emotional when she had a daydream experience and her imagination made it up. Faeries didn't exist, despite the fact that he was sitting across from one. He decides to move onto the only logical question he can think of at the moment. "So, should I go back to my room now then?" Tristan asks timidly.

"First of all, it's not your room. You are not moving in. Second, no one told you that you were exiled to the room, that was your own assumption so don't sound cross for your own imprisonment." Drake laces his voice with sarcasm.

Tristan rolls his eyes.

"I would really think twice before you make that move again," Drake's voice turns cold. "Do not underestimate me Tristan. Bait you may have been, but technically speaking you have served your purpose. I have no need for you anymore and I could care less what happens to you from here."

Tristan's paranoia about Calandra's well being all cross through his mind at once. He's been driving himself insane wondering what happened to her, where she is, and whether or not she's ok. "So, Calandra is here?" He asks hopeful.

"If by here you mean Faerie, then yes. She is with Jarreth though not me, of course." Drake answers and rolls his eyes.

Tristan's heart drops into his stomach. "How long have I been here exactly?"

"Just a few days." His answer is simple, as if it makes everything ok.

Tristan runs through all of the new information again in his head. Calandra is here and she is safe. But she is with Jarreth and he's not sure if that's of her own will or not. Here is Faerie, which moments ago, he had no clue even existed. The kicker was that despite how insane it all was, somehow he's not imagining any of this. Now he has to wonder if there really is something in his tea. Images of Alice in Wonderland flash through his head and he shakes them out.

"Why do you need Calandra?" Tristan finally figures out what piece of the puzzle that he is still missing.

"What do you mean?" Drake sounds as if his question makes no sense at all.

"You said I was bait, that you weren't sure if Jarreth did his job right and you had to make sure she came. Why do you need her? What is she to you?"

"A pawn really, more or less." Drake rolls his eyes and seems more than a little irritated by the turn in the conversation. "It's not that I need her, get that straight!" His eyes flash red and return to lavender almost immediately. "Faerie needs her apparently and I was simply ensuring that she got here one way or another."

Tristan picks up his teacup again and takes a sip. "So, I don't have to stay in the room?"

"Not at all Tristan." Drakes voice picks up a few notches of enthusiasm as if he is grateful that the questioning on Calandra is over. "You don't even have to stay in the house if you do not wish. Though you should probably think twice, or maybe even three times, about trying to meet with Calandra just yet. And do remember that you are in Faerie, so don't think for a second that you can do so without me knowing. Also, do not make the mistake of crossing me. It will not be pretty at all, that much I can assure you."

"I can't see her?" Tristan's mood drops down at least 50 levels.

"In due time you will. Plus, I didn't say you can't, I am just suggesting that you not seek her out. When the time is right, she will come to you, simple as that, take that for what it's worth." He shrugs.

Tristan finishes the rest of his tea in a single gulp and puts the cup back on the table. He crosses his arms across his chest as he processes what Calandra could possibly mean to Faerie. "On that note, I think I'll go out." Tristan says suddenly. He's not sure he actually wants to explore, but he defiantly knows he wants out of Drake's presence.

"As you wish." Drake stands and starts to walk out of the room. He pauses in the doorway and turns back to Tristan. "Keep in mind Tristan that you can not leave Faerie until I allow you to and that time is not now. Remember what I said about Calandra as well. It will do you well to listen to me, though I know you teenage humans have a tendency to not do so." Drake rolls his eyes, "Calandra has far more important things to deal with now, and trust me when I say that you can not fulfill her needs any longer."

Drake walks out of the room and disappears, he leaves Tristan alone on the couch as he tries to process everything and wonders what could cause Calandra to not want him anymore.

Chapter 13
What is Love?

"Jarreth, please!" Calandra whines as she pokes her bottom lip out slightly. "I want to see the town, it's the least you could do with everything you're expecting out of me!" She looks over to the dragonfly on her shoulder to reiterate her point.

Jarreth squirms on the couch next to her.

He looks at her, slightly aggravated, but he can't completely hide the humor behind it.

Calandra brings her gaze back to him and bats her eyelashes. "Come on! It'll be fun!" She laces her voice with as much sugar as she can possibly drum up.

The electricity shoots through her immediately. It starts in the center of the dragonfly, where Jarreth places his finger, and slowly courses through her. A smile crosses her face as she realizes she is getting what she wants.

"You might want to cover that up so we don't have the same reaction as the last time you were in town." He says as he removes his finger from her shoulder and Calandra readjusts to the absence of the currents.

Something about this place makes her brave. Maybe it's the comfort of having a part of something that belonged to her mother, mixed with the powers she's been discovering ever since coming to Faerie. Whatever the reasoning behind it is, Calandra has found herself being quite the daring person that she never was in the mortal world. A new confidence seems to have found her at being marked upon her arrival, and she's relishing in every moment of it and allowing herself to do and say things that she never would have before. It gives her even more of a sense of belonging to discover that here she can be the person she used to be only in her head.

"Because everyone doesn't already know who I am— mark exposed or not Jarreth. Drake's been out and I am sure he's filled everyone in anyways." She rolls her eyes at the mention of Drake. He has Tristan, she knows this somewhere deep down, but since he's assured Jarreth that Tristan is in no danger and isn't even being held against his will so to speak, she's put that issue on the back burner for now.

Drake, on the other hand, stays on the very front burner with the highest flame possible underneath— according to Jarreth that is. Calandra hasn't had a chance to interact with him much and she doesn't really like to judge people before giving them at least half a chance. Jarreth seems to have quite the distaste for Drake and

Calandra has been unable to figure out exactly why so far. His explanations tend to come out as riddles, and Calandra has yet to find a way to get the entire truth out of him. Frustrating as it has become, she has resolved to putting the truth train on hold for a while and focus more on figuring out the ins and outs of the world she finds herself a part of now.

"Regardless, I'd rather you put on a jacket or something at least." Jarreth breaks her from her thoughts.

"Does that mean you'll take me?" She suddenly lights up as she pieces together the words he doesn't actually say.

Jarreth nods simply and looks away from her. "I still don't think it's a good idea, mind you, but if it makes you quit whining, then yes I'll take you." His voice sounds defeated and guarded somehow.

Calandra smiles, victory traces in her voice. "In that case, I will go change my shirt." She heads up the narrow stairs disguised as a cupboard feeling quite proud of herself. Upon exploring the little tree house she had discovered a nice selection of clothes and jewelry left in the room form her mother as well as a few random hygiene products and some personal items as well. It was convenient and sentimental, which made it a win-win situation.

The third time is apparently the charm when it comes to convincing Jarreth to do something your way. She can't remember exactly what her tactics had been the other two times she had tried to convince him to take her into town, but she has now vowed to remember to try the guilt trip from the start if she ever needs to talk him into something again. Something in her gut tells her she probably will. She pulls a dark blue short sleeve shirt on over the pink spaghetti strap shirt she's been wearing. She looks in the mirror and decides to put a tad of makeup on to bring some color to her face. Stress must be making her look even paler than usual.

She takes a final glance at herself before she leaves the room. Calandra realizes this is the first time since she arrived and received the mark on her shoulder that she's covered it up. To her surprise, she has managed to grow rather fond of her dragonfly warrior, as she has decided to start calling it. Now that she can't look over and see it there on her shoulder, as it proudly watches over her, she feels a twinge of fear and uncertainty. Calandra shakes her head free of the emotions that threaten to take over her good mood, takes a deep breath, and heads back out to the living room. Jarreth still sits on the couch, in the same position he was in when she left.

"Not changing your mind are you?" Calandra asks from behind the couch. She expected to startle him since he hadn't acknowledged her return to the room, but as usual, Jarreth is completely unaffected.

"No dear, just still thinking it's not the best of ideas." He turns to face her, "I can feel your emotions coming into the room, so yes, I know you're here even if I don't see you." His smile turns slightly mischievous.

Jarreth has an uncanny way of somehow knowing what she's thinking even though he says feeling emotions is the only thing he does. Calandra sometimes has to wonder if he's also hiding a mind reading affinity as well. She walks around to the front of the couch and realizes that while she was getting ready, he got the pink liquid out. He has been spending enough time at the tree house that he brought a bottle over to have around, just in case. Calandra is actually starting to feel that he may be spending too much time there. Regardless of her now daring self, she's yet to be able to bring that subject up to him.

"So, are you going to tell me what that stuff is one day?" She asks as she guards her voice from the curiosity she feels about the shots he takes.

"It's nothing to concern yourself with." Jarreth says simply as he downs another shot of the stuff and closes the bottle back up tightly. "Ready to go?"

Calandra nods and the anticipation grows inside of her. Her mind travels back to her first trip through the town of Faerie. She was walking with someone she didn't know, wondering if she was being willingly kidnapped. The entire town was staring at the new mark on her shoulder and talking once she walked past. She still finds herself wondering what they were saying exactly. She is sure Drake has been saying things around town, so she has no clue what to expect this time around. But regardless of what she may see, she knows she needs to get to know this world and the heart of it is the town. She takes a deep breath as she readies herself for whatever may come from this escapade. *You asked for it,* she reminds herself.

An electric current runs through her and shoots all of her anxiety down in an instant when Jarreth puts his arm around her. "Come on, I'm right here with you." He smiles and leads her out the door.

"And will you actually answer my questions this time?" She asks as they begin their walk into town, Jarreth doesn't release his embrace on her.

"Have I quit answering your questions yet?" He asks, his voice is laced with concern.

"No."

"I just wanted to get things out in the open in private the first day Calandra, I wasn't trying to keep anything from you. I just figured a private location was more appropriate for what we had to discuss at that point."

Calandra sighs.

"I want you to trust me," Jarreth continues, "I need for you to trust me Calandra. There is—something more, another aspect to you balancing the world here. I'm not sure if you're ready to hear it yet or not, but I think it's something you need to know before you delve too far into our world."

Calandra feels her heart drop down to the ground. In the last few days, she had come a long way in accepting where she is and what they are asking of her. She still isn't anywhere close to making a commitment to anything, but she's starting to come to terms to what may lay ahead of her if she does. But she has at least begun to relax, to accept it, and to allow herself to trust her own instincts. And much to her surprise, she's begun to find herself enjoying where she is and she has even somewhat been enjoying Jarreth's company. Now the question is, does she actually want to hear something that might possibly undo all of that?

"Is it bad?" She finally manages to ask.

"Not really bad, it's just something you should know before you get too far into any decision making." Jarreth tightens his grip on her shoulder as he says it and the electricity intensifies through her.

"So it's not going to send me running for the hills?" She asks with heat rising to her cheeks.

"Well I certainly hope not!" But there is fear in his voice as he says it.

Calandra takes a steadying breath and looks around. They are walking through the small path in the woods that leads from the town to Jarreth's house. Calandra knows they will arrive into town shortly, which means its do or die time.

"Okay, shoot," She says finally and relishes in the feel of Jarreth's touch to take the edge off of her anxiety.

"There are things that tie into magic and

power to make it more powerful. Love is the greatest power in the world, whether it be mortal or Fae. Tie love and magic together and you create an unstoppable force." Jarreth continues to walk without taking his embrace from her, but his explanation is apparently over.

Calandra stops and stares at him, pushing for more. "What does that tell me?" She scoffs. "Really Jarreth, the riddles do get old after a while."

"I told you, they aren't riddles. I'm trying to entice you to figure it out for yourself. Just put the pieces together Cal." He smiles wickedly.

"I've had a tough day, come on!" She whines.

"Oh no." Jarreth laughs and taps her nose playfully. "You've already pulled that excuse once and I caved, it's not gonna happen again. I've given you all the information you need."

"So love somehow effects whether I can actually fix things here or not?" She is frustrated, but concludes that she isn't going to get anything else out of him, so she doesn't waste her breath pushing it further.

He nods, "it could possibly have everything to do with it."

Calandra begins to walk again and Jarreth follows suit.

"You think that's all there is to it? Simple as that?" Jarreth finally asks as they break through the woods and find the town in front of them.

Calandra looks at him bewildered. "There's more?"

Jarreth chuckles. "Oh, you have so much to learn about Faerie." His smile lingers and touches every crevice on his face. It is an amazing sight to see and Calandra can't help but to smile back.

Jarreth walks her into a small bar with old saloon style doors. Calandra stops to admire the mixture of centuries that make up this town. Some things look like they are from an old western movie, some Victorian, some modern, it's a more than fascinating combination.

"What is this place?" She asks as Jarreth leads her to a small booth in the back corner.

"Just a little bar." He shrugs it off.

"Um—" Calandra bites her lip and leaves the rest of her sentence hanging.

Jarreth stares at her and waits for her to say something more. "Trying out one of my riddles are we?" He chuckles as he snaps his fingers at the blonde behind the bar counter.

"It's just that— I'm not actually old enough to drink." She finally finishes her sentence and ends it with her face crimson red. She decides not to mention that she doesn't want to drink regardless of her age. She has an unsettling feeling in the pit of her stomach being in a place like this.

Jarreth laughs. "There's not exactly a legal age in Faerie dear."

The bar tender arrives at the table and looks inquisitively at Calandra. "What can I do you for today Jare?" She finally asks, her eyes don't leave Calandra.

"One of my usuals, surprise me." He says then looks to Calandra. "And for you?"

Calandra stares blankly at him, unsure of what she's supposed to say or do. She knows she doesn't want to drink, but she doesn't want to come off as being quite so innocent either.

Jarreth chuckles at her as she stares blankly around and endeavors to decide what to say. Finally, he decides to save her and looks up at Glyda. "She'll have a strawberry tea. He says and waves his hand at her to shoo her off.

Calandra blushes with embarrassment. "So—" She decides to change the subject in hopes of not discussing it. "I take it you come here often?"

"What gave you that impression?"

"Well, she has a nickname for you, and you have multiple usuals."

"So you can put things together for yourself!" Jarreth smiles, "you wanna try again for what we were talking about on the way here in that case?" He stares intently at her and the bartender returns with their drinks. Jarreth's is a shot glass with a dark green liquid in it.

"Oh— right." She relents back to the conversation from the walk into town and takes a sip of her tea. It's sweet but tart and it warms her throat as it slides down.

Jarreth continues to stare intently at her, to pressure her to figure it out and also to make it clear he isn't going to help her in any way.

She takes another sip of her drink. "So you're really gonna be no help at all?" She decides to try a pout again. After all, it did work to get her into town, maybe it'll help her out again.

"I don't think so Cal!" Jarreth takes his shot and holds the glass in the air to signal the bartender to get him another one. "You only get to make me cave so many times and you've reached your limit for the day!" A wicked smile crosses his face as Glyda returns with a new shot, this one is a baby blue liquid.

Love is the greatest power in the world, mortal or Fae, tie love and magic together and you create an unstoppable force. The words come back to her mind and she tries to dissect them as she sips on her drink and begins to feel braver with every sip she takes.

"So, what? I have to be in love?" She finally starts to bring her thoughts to words.

"You're getting there."

"Getting to being in love?" Maybe it's the pressure of her surroundings, but her thoughts are staring to cloud together and they aren't making complete sense.

"You already are, aren't you!?" Tristan's voice makes her and Jarreth both jump.

Jarreth's eyes flash purple momentarily and a smile crosses his face.

"Well, yeah— I mean, not that— I—" She can't make herself manage an actual sentence. Thoughts fly through her head and make her feel a little dizzy. She does love Tristan, doesn't she? Noting seems to make much sense anymore and her emotions have been on overdrive ever since she came to Faerie. She frowns slightly and strives to figure out something coherent to say. "Where did you come from?"

"Nice to see you too!" Tristan is offended and looks skeptically between Calandra and Jarreth.

Jarreth places his hand on top of hers in the middle of the table and smiles reassuringly.

"Just keep going with your thinking there."

Calandra goes back to her train of thought somewhat thankful Jarreth doesn't want to continue that particular conversation further, especially now that Tristan has surprised them with his presence. Love. Love and magic. Unstoppable force. Think Calandra, think.

"Who I love..." Calandra says shocked as it falls into place, "it matters who I love?"

Jarreth nods.

"But how? Why?"

"Because—" An unfamiliar voice answers and Jarreth's eyes flash red and his expression turns grim. Calandra turns to see Drake standing next to her. "Two and two equals four right?" He grins as he sits down in the booth with her and Tristan and makes everyone uncomfortable.

"Drake." Jarreth says, his voice much colder than Calandra has heard from him.

"Jarreth." Drake returns his tone and turns his attention back to Calandra.

Calandra takes a large gulp of her drink in hopes it will help to calm her nerves. For some reason, she feels like she's in the middle of some sort of territory marking contest. It's a rather uncomfortable place to be and she wishes for the comforting electricity of Jarreth's touch suddenly.

"Yes." She says finally ready to break the awkward silence.

"Yes what?" Drake says.

"Yes, two and two is four. Your point being?" Calandra's sarcasm comes more willingly than she expects it to.

"My point being, wouldn't it make sense then that power on top of power equals more power?" Drake snaps his fingers in the air to call the bartender over to the table.

Glyda looks more than happy to oblige Drake's request. She glides over to the table with a flirtatious grin on her face, her eyes burn straight into Drake. *Obvious much?* Calandra thinks and then instantly wonders why it matters to her.

Glyda's hand goes straight to Drake's shoulder when she reaches the table and he puts his on top of hers. Calandra's entire body tenses in response. Calandra looks immediately to Tristan and hopes he doesn't notice. Luckily for her, he is too busy giving Jarreth a death stare to be paying her any attention.

"The usual please." Drake runs his hand slowly over Glyda's hand as he says it.

"Another for me— something stronger." Jarreth says, his eyes still not moving from Drake.

"And me too!" Calandra looks at Glyda and gives her the best evil look she can muster. She's never really done the whole glare at someone and make them wish they were dead thing before, but she feels confident with what she manages to come up with. Glyda squirms in response and Calandra feels proud of herself, until she sees the smile on Drake's face and realizes she may be giving him exactly what he wants. Calandra frowns at the realization and quickly gulps down the rest of her drink as Glyda walks away for their order.

"Anyways," Drake continues as if nothing happened, "basically, you will be a powerful person on your own Calandra. Because of what you are, and because of this—" his finger graces slowly across Calandra's shoulder where the dragonfly is covered by her clothing and Tristan jolts as straight as a board. "If you were with another powerful Faerie, say— Jarreth." Drake scoffs and rolls his yes as he says it. "Or me.." His eyes gleam and his smile turns wicked. "The combination of powers on top of the power and magic from love, well— it'd be quite an extraordinary thing to see."

"Hello?" Tristan finally breaks into the conversation. "She's not exactly up for grabs." He places his arm possessively around Calandra's arm and she shrinks down feeling more than a little embarrassed.

Glyda returns with the drinks. She places another strawberry tea in front of Calandra but doesn't look at her. She puts a shot of the familiar pink swirling liquid in front of Jarreth. In front of Drake, she puts a strange silver contraption, a long silver lighter, and a brown bottle.

"Anything else?" She places her hand over Drake's shoulder. Calandra fights against her instinct to react and distracts herself by looking at Jarreth.

"That's all for now." Drake brushes Glyda off, he suddenly seems completely uninterested. Calandra wonders if it has anything to do with the fact that she kept her reactions hidden or if she's simply flattering herself with that train of thought. Once again, she wonders why she even cares.

"What someone isn't telling you." Jarreth finally takes his glare from Drake and turns to face Calandra. His face is still stiff, but his eyes seem softer. "Is that not only will the person you're with effect how powerful you become, but it will also directly effect the amount of good or evil in you." Jarreth takes his shot quickly and holds the glass up in the air for another one. "But, you're a smart girl Cal, we can trust you to make the right decision." Jarreth's eyes narrow in Drake's direction.

"There isn't a decision to be made!" Tristan corrects.

Calandra takes a long gulp of her new drink and tries to drown out the situation going on around her. She decides she doesn't want to respond to or even look at anyone at the moment. The amount of pressure that has just been laid on her makes her head spin. Calandra still feels Jarreth's gaze on her. He is watching her, probably trying to gauge her reaction or feel her emotions. She tries to shut him out completely but isn't sure how to tell whether she's successful or not.

In an effort to distract herself and resist the temptation to look at Jarreth, she decides to turn her attention to Drake. He has lit a small burner at the bottom of the silver contraption and is now opening the brown bottle. He places the lid next to him and pours a thick, dark crimson liquid into the triangular glass that sits on top. At once, the liquid begins to bubble and flames blue for a few seconds before going out. Using mostly his long, angled, brittle fingernails, Drake picks up the cup and gulps down the liquid quickly before he starts the routine again. Calandra watches in amazement and curiosity takes over any other thoughts or emotions she had.

"I take it you haven't explained all of our ways to her." Drake's voice pulls her out of her daze and he nods his head towards her.

Calandra clears her throat, returns to her drink, and tries to hide her blush. She finally makes herself look up at Jarreth questioningly. Jarreth smiles at her reassuringly and somehow she figures it means he'll explain later. She bats her eyelashes at him. He shakes his head no slightly and tries to stifle a laugh.

"Well, well, well—" Drake breaks up the silent communication going on between them. "Looks like you two are already starting to bond, eh?" He takes the shot of the red liquid he's just prepared and snaps his fingers for Glyda to return.

Tristan looks between Calandra and Jarreth again with hurt and confusion on his face.

Without saying anything further, Drake motions for Glyda to take his stuff from the table and gets up. He slowly brushes his arm across Glyda's back and smiles at Calandra as he does. Her body stiffens, she returns to her drink, and finishes it in one big gulp. "I told you not to search her out just yet Tristan, I knew you wouldn't listen." He winks and turns and walks out of the bar.

"Another!" Calandra says before Glyda can walk away. "Well, he's charming isn't he?" Calandra says after Glyda leaves.

"No!" Jarreth says rather harshly.

"Relax, it was a joke. You know, a bit of sarcasm."

"I knew that." Jarreth's voice turns slightly defensive.

"Yeah, ok," Calandra laughs.

Glyda returns with their drinks. "That'll be all for today," Jarreth tells her and gulps his shot down. "We'll be leaving shortly, put it on my tab."

"And Drake's as well?" Glyda asks with a smile.

Jarreth rolls his eyes. "And Drake's too I guess."

Calandra sucks down her drink while Jarreth stares at her. "What?" She asks finally.

"Nothing, just thinking." He says as he

places his hand behind his head and leans back slightly in the booth.

"About?"

"Don't fall for Drake's tricks Calandra. He's not exactly— good." His face is serious and the expression looks out of place with the rest of his body in such a relaxed position.

"According to someone that knows you pretty well, neither are you." She points out.

Jarreth chuckles and nods. "This is true."

"Does anyone want to fill me in on all of this?" Tristan chimes in.

Calandra finds herself surprised that she seems to have forgotten that he was there. "It's— well, complicated!" Calandra finishes her drink.

"Come, let's go," Jarreth smiles as he stands up and holds his hand out for her.

"Where exactly are we going?" Tristan stands in front of Jarreth and holds his hand out for Calandra.

"I can handle myself thank you!" She says as she stands up quickly out of the booth in an attempt to make a point. But in the dramatic effort to make a point, her foot catches on the leg of the table beneath her and she looses her balance and falls towards the floor.

Jarreth reaches his arm out and steadies her. "You sure about that Cal?" He chuckles.

Tristan's glare burns into Jarreth.

Calandra's entire face turns red and she shakes it no.

Tristan puts his arm around her waist to keep her steady and walks her out of the bar. "Lucky you have me for support huh?"

"Too bad you have no idea where we're going." Jarreth mumbles under his breath.

They turn out of the bar and head back towards the tree house.

"What? The bar is the only thing in town?" She asks when she realizes her exploration day is over.

"No, but I think you've had enough for the day. The sun is going down, your boyfriend has returned and I feel obligated to get you home now." Jarreth walks a little further ahead of them and out of earshot.

Calandra throws her head back and laughs heartily, though she is unsure of why the statement is so funny.

Tristan leans into her. "Nice to see you too Cal, glad to know you missed me."

The pressure fills her head again as she realizes this cannot end well for anyone.

****

Jarreth, Tristan, and Calandra sit on the couch in his little cabin. Jarreth has his bottle of pink liquid out on the table and two shot glasses. He pours some into each of the glasses.

"Two?" Calandra says as she pulls herself out of the swirling thoughts in her head and realizes what he's doing.

"Both for me, don't sound so excited." He chuckles.

Tristan watches them both carefully. In an effort to ignore the tension building in the room, Calandra straightens up with an idea. "That, I believe, is where you're wrong!" She says and in one swift movement she grabs one of the glasses and gulps down the liquid before Jarreth can stop her.

It's sweet and a little sticky, but it doesn't burn at all. It is thick and soothing as it slides down. Something familiar swims in her as she drinks it, but she can't quite put her finger on it. She puts the glass back down on the table and smiles daringly at Jarreth.

He simply stares at her, shocked. "Well played dear, well played." He chuckles as he takes his own shot.

"So, now that I've had it, are you going to tell me what it is?"

"I think not. Let that be a lesson for you to not drink or eat things that you have no idea what they are. Especially in Faerie dear, we're not all as innocent as I am." He winks.

"Somehow I doubt that."

"What? You think they are all innocent?" Jarreth now has alarm on his face.

"No, I doubt that you are that innocent." She laughs and points at the shot glasses.

"This is true." He frowns slightly and refills the glasses. "However, comparatively, I'm not so bad really."

"Compared to who?" Calandra giggles.

Tristan scoffs and goes upstairs to the room. He had been less than uncomfortable since he came strolling back into the scene unexpectedly. Calandra has a feeling he had expected Jarreth to leave when they got to the tree house. To be honest, Calandra had expected him to as well, but he didn't, and she wasn't going to push the issue.

"Others here I guess." He shrugs and hands her another glass. "Seriously though Calandra, what Drake was telling you, the amount of power and evil in the person that you choose to love directly effects the person you will become and in turn, what this world becomes."

"Why do I feel like there's a warning in there?" She asks and shoots the liquid back.

"Because there is," he begins as he takes his own drink. "If you fall in love with evil, this world is history. There's your warning, without a riddle even!"

"No pressure or anything though right?"

Calandra chuckles and lays her head back on the couch as the drinks begin to make her vision swirl together.

"None at all," he whispers, "You don't need any pressure, I can take it away."

Calandra's entire body freezes just as her emotions start to drain out of her, thanks to Jarreth. "No, I don't think you can." She says simply and sits up straight. "I think you need to go. I need to go talk to Tristan."

Jarreth's eyes flash green and return to baby blue again. Without a single word, he stands and leaves the tree house. Calandra sighs at the turn of events the day managed to take. Tristan is upstairs upset and clearly they have some things to discuss. Too many emotions clutter her head and she feels like she may explode. Calandra sighs audibly and leans back on the couch and closes her eyes to the entire situation.

Chapter 14
Possibilities

"So, you've been holding up well in my absence I see." Tristan says as Calandra sets a plate in front of him.

Jarreth's body has gone stiff and he is sitting over his plate with his fork in his hand in midair, but he's yet to take a bite. Calandra had managed to pass out on the couch last night instead of going to talk to Tristan, which made things awkward, to say the least. To make matters even worse, Jarreth showed up first thing this morning before she had even woken up, which left things beyond awkward. Calandra isn't even sure where Tristan stayed and somehow she feels that would be the wrong question to ask. Calandra smiles timidly at Tristan and shoots a quick glance over at Jarreth. The room feels as if it is filled with pressure and at any moment it might combust.

"How have you been?" Calandra finally slices through the room with a question for Tristan.

In typical teenage boy style, Tristan is already shoveling food down his throat. Regardless of any life situation or drama going on, a boy still has to eat! Jarreth watches him in shock, his own fork still in midair.

With food still in his mouth, Tristan responds. "As good as can be expected I guess."

"So you're haven't been, like, tied up in a dungeon or anything apparently," Jarreth's voice sounds cold and Calandra shoots a glare at him.

Tristan quits eating and cuts a look at Jarreth. "No, I'm not. I've been kept in a tiny room, but when I finally left Drake told me I didn't have to stay in there. Although he did suggest I not come looking for Calandra. But here I am— and here you are." Tristan looks back at Calandra. "So does he actually stay at his house at all? He does have one, right?" He says he with an extra dose of hate and tilts his head towards Jarreth.

"Of course he has his own house Tristan." Calandra feels the temperature rise in the air around her as the pressure turns up a few notches.

"And yet— he's here." Once again Tristan puts an emphasis on the word he and he shoots Jarreth a sideways glance.

Jarreth's body tenses, his eyes flash red, but he doesn't say anything.

"Yes Tristan, he's here, trying to help me with things."

"Hmm," Tristan scoffs.

"So, why exactly don't you just go home?"

Jarreth finally breaks his own silence. The question is directed at Tristan, but he doesn't look at him. He finally starts in on his own breakfast.

Calandra simply plays with her own food, she pushes it around on the plate with her fork, unable to actually make herself eat.

"I can't go home for one," Tristan has a very matter-of-fact tone to his voice. "Even if Drake would let me, I'm not leaving without Calandra."

Jarreth opens his mouth to say something and Calandra drops her fork and holds her hand out to stop him. She shakes her head at him and cuts him a look. Jarreth fights to take in a breath and stops himself. Tristan looks at Jarreth suspiciously and turns curious when he looks at Calandra.

"It's— complicated." She says simply and looks back at her plate.

"Dang it Calandra!" Tristan slams his fork onto his plate and pushes it away. "What is wrong with you?"

Calandra looks up at him with her jaw dropped. He's never lost his cool with her before, she's never even seen him angry before. They've never argued, nothing more than merely teasing each other and roughhousing. This new side of him cuts a slit through her heart and allows everything to bleed out slowly.

Jarreth's entire body tenses and he finally drops his fork that he's been holding midair during the majority of the morning conversation. "I—" His voice is harsh and his eyes have yet to change back to their normal blue yet, they are staying red for longer than Calandra's ever seen them. "I will NOT have you come into this house and talk to her like that!" Jarreth stares at Tristan with an intensity Calandra's never seen in anyone before. Part of her expects Tristan to spontaneously combust from the glare.

Calandra lets out a breath and forces her powers to will her to focus on the here and now. She holds up an index finger to Jarreth and walks over to the cabinet where he's chosen to stash his mystery juice. She pulls out a shot glass and the bottle of pink liquid. Too many emotions from all of the drama she's caused pulse through her when she looks at it and she has to remind herself to focus on the task at hand. Keep Jarreth and Tristan from killing each other, she tells herself. She shakes her head to clear her mind and turns and heads back to the bar. Tristan is watching her carefully, a disgusted look on his face. She gives a slight smile to him and then steps right in between the two of them. She pours a shot of the liquid, which reminds her that she still has no idea what it actually is, and places it in front of Jarreth. He is still looking around her to stare at Tristan, who is squirming in his seat under the intense glare.

Calandra moves to the side to catch Jarreth's gaze and clears her throat. As if he's been pulled out of a trance, Jarreth responds and looks a bit lost but he focuses on Calandra. She nods her head towards the shot glass she's placed in front of him. "Drink and chill!" She scolds.

Jarreth looks as if he's going to challenge her momentarily, but instead he takes a breath and turns in his chair until he is no longer facing Tristan and takes back the shot. He keeps his head turned up momentarily with his eyes closed, enjoying it more than Calandra has seen him do before, the motion reminds her of Drake and makes her feel uncomfortable. He finally turns his head back up and slams the glass on the bar. Calandra taps his hand a few times and pushes the bottle closer to him to signal him to have more if he needs it. She then turns to face Tristan, who is giving her his own scornful look.

"It's just— I need to be here Tristan. People here, well, they need me." She tries to think of a way to put it all into a statement that makes sense, but she can't seem to find the words. She tries to think of a way to lessen the blow that she may never return to the mortal world, that he should probably just go home, start all over and forget all about her. She quickly realizes she can't say any of it without crying, so she decides against it.

"And what about the people at home who need you?" Tristan's voice is quiet, he is hurt.

"No one needs me Tristan, not there."

"Your dad—" Tristan looks down at the bar in front of him before he continues. "Me."

Calandra sighs heavily. How was she supposed to do this again? It seemed like a much easier task when it was just an idea in her head, but now that she's actually started, it seems significantly harder. She focuses her powers up around her once more, and feels the comfort their presence offers. She is beginning to be thankful for the powers she has received, even though they are limited, she has discovered they are especially nice for times that you don't want to feel things.

"My dad, I'm quite sure could care less at this point where I end up or if he sees me again." Calandra looks away and begins twisting her fingers into each other. "You can go home without me Tristan, there's no reason for you to stay here." She suddenly feels torn in half. There are two separate people on either side of her and she wants to find a way to please both of them, yet Tristan is going to get hurt and she knows it deep down. Judging by the look on his face and his shallow breathing, he seems to know it too.

"I can't leave yet anyways. I'm not exactly tied and bound type kidnapped, but I do still have limits," Tristan says. "So, what, you're never coming home then?" The look on his face when he says it is a mixture of hurt and confusion. Calandra's heart bursts open and a spurt of blood pours out.

Calandra looks down at the bar, unable to form a single word. She opens her mouth, then closes it again. She sighs and decides instead to pick up Tristan's plate as a distraction. She walks over to the sink with it and begins cleaning it.

"Well, that answers that I guess." Tristan mumbles, "I assume YOU encouraged this." He turns to face Jarreth.

"If you mean encouraged her to follow her destiny and do what she's meant to, then yes I did. You can't make me feel guilty for it either, so don't waste your breath." Jarreth pours himself another shot without so much as looking at Tristan.

"What she's meant to do or what you want

her to do? The two seem to be quite different."

Calandra finally decides the plate is more than spotless and that she should focus on mediating the debate that is heating up around her. She turns to see Jarreth gulping down a shot and then immediately pouring himself a new one.

"What she's meant to do Tristan. Do not come here and chastise me. Need I remind you that you are in Faerie and you ought not to mess with beings you do not understand. It will get you in more trouble than you'd know what to do with." Jarreth takes a breath and takes his shot. Calandra notices that his eyes are still red. "Now would you like to continue this battle or return to your prison?"

"Need I remind you that I never left here, you're the one who came over this morning and ruined the day." Tristan's voice holds confidence but his face doesn't show any.

"Ok." Calandra finally decides it's time to fully intervene. She walks around the bar where she can get a good look at the both of them. She turns to face Jarreth first. "You, take one more drink and then I think you need to go and leave us alone." She gives him a look to signify that he doesn't need to challenge her at the moment. She takes a breath to get a little more courage and then turns to face Tristan. "And you—" she begins in on him, "do need to learn exactly who you are dealing with before you wind up getting yourself killed Tristan, just saying. I know that Drake has much less patience than Jarreth does."

Calandra hears the shot glass slam down onto the bar next to her again and realizes Jarreth has already taken his shot. He places his arm on her back and sends a shock of electricity through her, her body naturally caves into the shock and she smiles in response. Tristan tenses.

"I'll be around when you're finished if you decide you need me." Jarreth tells her, his eyes are finally back to their gorgeous shade of baby blue. He stops next to Tristan's chair as he passes by. "Don't think I won't know if she needs assistance just because I'm not where you can see me."

Confusion crosses Tristan's face.

"Faerie," Jarreth explains, "seriously, learn something of it if you plan to survive in this world for long." Jarreth rolls his eyes before he strolls out of the kitchen.

The pressure in the room drops drastically once Jarreth is gone. Calandra sighs in relief and a hope rises in her that maybe the rest of this conversation can go over slightly decently. Hopefully a bit more like the way she has been planning in her head.

"So what?" Tristan breaks the silence unexpectedly. "You're just gonna let him come back over once you're done dealing with me?"

"Is that really the question you want to go into right now?" Calandra asks trying to shy away from the hurt that is plainly written on Tristan's face. She can't deal with that right now.

"No", he sighs, "I guess it's not, but I believe I have my answer regardless." Tristan looks away and Calandra sits in the stool that Jarreth left abandoned.

"Listen." Calandra finally figures out how to form full sentences again. "Things are just—" the ability abandons her almost instantly.

"Complicated?" Tristan finishes for her. "Yeah, you said that already."

"I'm sorry that you got pulled into all of this Tristan. I think that's all I can really say."

"Sorry? After all we've been through together and now all of this, that's the best you have for me?"

"It's just that I belong here now Tristan." Calandra adjusts herself nervously in her chair. "I can't leave, it's just that simple."

"That's not simple at all Calandra! You have a life, we had a life, just in case you've already forgotten about it." Tristan stands up and moves in front of Calandra. "Look, I can see you have your own thing going on here and I guess I shouldn't have come." He runs his hand through his hair to brush it from his face. "I take it you know where to find me should you desire to do so. Do what you need to do here I guess, but don't forget that you had a life and people who cared for you before this place. This isn't the only place you belong."

"I really am sorry Tristan. I wish you could've been left out of all of this." Calandra's heart has completely bled out around her now and she's having trouble breathing.

"Don't be." He surprises her with his response. "I would have driven myself insane wondering what in the world happened to you." Tristan places his hand very lightly on her cheek. Calandra fights the urge to lean into it. "At least this way I know what happened to you." Tristan smiles his heartbreakingly gorgeous smile and turns and walks off. He stops in the doorway that connects the kitchen and the living room and turns to face her once more.

"You know Cali, you're the one that's hung the sun and the moon in my world for a while now. All I ever wanted was to do the same for you, and I tried, I really did. But I think you've always been meant to do more then make the world for just one person. I think I've known that for a while now." His eyes glisten over and he looks away to straighten up before he continues. "I think you've been looking in all the wrong places trying to find your meaning in life. If you would have just looked up, you could have found your significance without any of this. Either way, I hope you find your something more Cal, I really do. At least if I'm still part of this world then I can still be a part of you, even if it turns out to not be in the same way that I planned." His mouth opens once more but before anything comes out, he closes it, and turns and walks away again. She hears the door close behind him and suddenly realizes there is a new emptiness inside of her.

She needs Tristan. He has become her everything over the time they've been together. He's been the one to help her out of her shell. He has stood beside her with all of her father's drama. Every fight, every cry, every happy moment, she has turned to Tristan through it all. That was before, she tells herself. Now is different. Now has to be different. Faerie is a new world and she can feel herself morphing into a new person, one that she feels comfortable with. Something about this new road just feels right, finally. She has to keep pushing through despite what may come her way, she knows that. The things from before have been to make her into the person that she needed to be to get to this place. Now it's time to see what she can become.

Regardless of her own selfish thoughts and reasons for staying, Tristan deserves better. Calandra commits to confront Drake and make him let Tristan go. With a new outlook and resolve on what she must do, Calandra stands from the barstool and decides the mess of the dishes can wait a while.

Chapter 15
Lies

"Absolutely not!" Drake's eyes have darkened considerably since Calandra began her explanation of what she wants from him. "If you really thought that I would go for this then someone hasn't done a very good job of telling you about me." Drake shoots a glance at Jarreth who sits in the corner of the room, hidden in shadows.

Jarreth hasn't said much since Calandra told him she wanted him to bring her to Drake's. He wasn't at all happy with the idea. Actually, that was an understatement, he was angry when she first brought it up and refused to talk about it at all for a bit. Calandra had tried the whole guilt trip and pouting scheme again, but it didn't work this time around. Instead she had to go about actually negotiating with him and explaining her reasons for needing to see Drake. He had still been reluctant, but in the end, he gave in, probably more in an effort to shut her up than anything.

Drake's house wasn't quite what she was expecting. Somehow she had pictured something comparative to a dungeon. It was actually similar to Jarreth's house, which creeped Calandra out more than just a little bit. There was less furniture and decorations in Drake's house than in Jarreth's. The dark curtains on every window seem to be up to purposely keep the light out, which gives off a creepy and depressing feel. The couch isn't comfortable in the least, but here she sits with Drake sitting too close for comfort, and Jarreth sulking in the corner, trying to hide his immaturity in the shadows.

Calandra hasn't had much interaction with Drake and what little she did have wasn't exactly pleasant, but she had to take a shot in the dark and attempt to make him let Tristan go home. She owed Tristan at least that much. He had already served his purpose, Calandra was here. She came in hoping that just simply explaining this would be enough to make Drake do as she requested. Obviously, she had been very wrong in that assumption.

"I don't understand why you need him anymore, I'm here aren't I?" She says.

"I didn't say that I needed him anymore. But that doesn't mean I'm finished or am willing to let him go." Drake shrugs as if this should be common sense.

Calandra feels her nerves start to rise at his attitude. How he could be so nonchalant about this, as if it should be his call what is done with Tristan, it seems to irk every nerve in her body.

She knows she needs to be calm in order to negotiate with him, so she centers herself on her power and pulls a calming sensation from it.

"Surely there's something we can do to work this out Drake." She can see Jarreth's body tense out of the corner of her eye as she says it.

Drake's eyes flash darker for a few moments and his smile turns quite devious. "Oh, I know there's something that I'd be willing to cave for. But I also know better than to think that it'll happen. You're wasting your time Calandra, not to say I don't enjoy seeing you sitting on my couch." Drake smirks.

Calandra resists the urge to roll her eyes. "What is it?" She asks after a few moments.

Drake seems to ignore her question. He looks over to Jarreth in the corner and they exchange a look that Calandra can't quite place. Jarreth's entire body tenses and his eyes change colors, although through the shadows, Calandra can't tell for sure what color. She does notice they go very dark. Drake's smile widens. Jarreth's fists clench and he stands up.

"That's enough!" He yells. "I told you this was pointless and we shouldn't have come." He still doesn't move from the corner.

"Oh, I wouldn't say it was a total waste!" Drake says coolly.

"Would you two stop it?" Calandra snaps. "You guys are worse than a bunch of hormone driven teenagers!" She isn't sure where this bravery was coming from exactly, it's so unlike her. "You!" she points her finger at Jarreth, "sit! I asked him a question and he is going to answer it." She turns her attention to Drake, and chooses to not even acknowledge the reaction that Jarreth must be giving her for standing up to him. Drake, on the other hand, looks quite pleased with her outbreak. "Wipe that smirk off your face and just answer the question!" she tells him. She holds tight to the confidence that is surging through her, afraid that if she doesn't hold onto it for dear life, it may disappear and never return.

Drake lifts an eyebrow at her, trying to gauge just how far she is willing to go with her new attitude. "Now this is a welcome change." He says, fighting the urge to let the smirk return.

Calandra rolls her eyes at him, making sure he knows she's beyond irritated and not in the mood to deal with the games. She's beginning to realize that games seem to go hand in hand with Drake and she probably should have been more prepared for something like this. Jarreth had mentioned that before they came. She pushes that thought away, she is too aggravated with him at the moment to admit to herself that perhaps she should have listened to him better.

Calandra is still wondering about the history between Drake and Jarreth. There is a hate there, she can see that. But despite her best efforts, she can't seem to get Jarreth to explain it to her. All she has been able to get out of Jarreth was that Drake wasn't a good guy. Anyone could see that, but there is a level of animosity between the two of them that has to be the result of something much deeper, something that Calandra desperately wants to know.

"I do not wish to discuss my terms in front of him." Drake breaks her from her thoughts and brings her back to the present. His eyes dart over to Jarreth, who has sat back down and is sulking once more.

"Well I'm not leaving, so tough." Jarreth responds, his face is now completely hidden in the shadows.

"Geez!" Calandra breaks down again. "How am I supposed to get anything accomplished here with you two constantly in a territorial contest around me?" She begins rubbing her left temple where the tension is building.

Drake laughs. Jarreth doesn't move a muscle, but Calandra is sure there is a pretty unpleasant look on his face at the moment, she chooses not to look.

"Fine!" She says standing up off the couch. "You can stay right there!" She says to Jarreth before turning to face Drake. "You and I will go in another room to discuss this."

Drake smiles, he is obviously more than pleased with this new suggestion and Calandra wonders if she's made a huge mistake. *Too late now,* she reminds herself. She tries to come up with a way out of the predicament she has created for herself, but she's left with nothing. The only option now is to just go with it. Suck it up and deal. She takes a deep breath, and pulls from her power to give her the strength to face what may be ahead. She refuses to look over at Jarreth. She doesn't want to see the look of disapproval she knows he must have.

Drake reaches his arm out to her. "Come my lady!" He smiles.

Calandra rolls her eyes. "How about you just lead the way and I'll follow?"

Drake sighs, "suit yourself." He walks off towards the next room.

Calandra finally dares to take a look back at Jarreth before she walks after Drake. She isn't at all prepared for what she sees. He's leaning enough that his face is out of the shadows and he isn't wearing an expression of disappointment or anger like she was expecting. There's nothing but hurt on his face. His eyes are a much darker shade of blue than usual, and he looks slightly broken. The strength that Calandra had been able to draw for herself deflates instantly. But she has to face this situation now, she started it and now she has to finish it. She takes a deep breath and gives Jarreth her best apology smile before she turns and follows after Drake.

There is a small hallway that leads from the living room to the bedroom Drake is heading towards. There is what Calandra assumes to be a closet door on one side and a black hutch on the other. Just as she's walking past the hutch and is about to step over the threshold into the bedroom after Drake, something catches her eye. The top of the hutch is covered in pictures, but there is one frame in particular that stops her dead in her tracks and sends her world finally spinning into the vast of space straight for a black hole. Calandra is unable to believe what she sees. She pulls the frame off of the hutch to get a better look at it and be sure her head isn't deceiving her.

"What is this?!" She asks, unable to pull her gaze from the picture in her hands.

It's the bar that Jarreth had taken her to the previous day. Standing in front of the bar are two men standing on each side of a petite woman. The man on the left is Drake, his hair is much shorter, but other than that he looks the same. The man on the right is Jarreth, other than having a simple and spiked hairstyle, he looks just the same as well. The woman in the middle is what throws Calandra off and makes her world flip to catastrophe mode completely. The woman is Calandra's mother, Hollyn.

The world seems to be spinning backwards, or maybe its just spinning too fast, something is defiantly off. Nothing makes sense. How do you... How does... she can't even make a coherent thought let alone manage to put together a sentence to question what she is looking at. Drake leans into the doorway next to her, his arms are crossed coyly, and he has a smirk on his face. Calandra notices him and feels the urge to remove that smirk herself, it's becoming quite the irritant.

She's still busy glaring at Drake and envisioning herself taking the look off his face when she feels the currents start to run through her. Jarreth's hand is on her back and the feeling radiates from that point throughout the rest of her body. She turns to face him, still lost on what to feel or think. There is a gray fog running through her mind.

"Cal," Jarreth says softly, "how about you come sit back down dear?"

"What is this?" She asks, searching his eyes for some sort of answer and finding nothing.

"Come sit down please." He repeats and pushes her towards the couch slightly.

She watches him, still feeling dazed, but walks back to the couch and takes a seat with the picture still in her hand.

"Drake." Jarreth suddenly sounds calm. "Go make her some tea, I'll handle the explanation."

"Of course you will." Drake replies without a change in his expression.

Jarreth's eyes flash red. "Just do it!" He turns away from Drake and slowly approaches the couch and takes the seat next to Calandra. His face is troubled, broken. It's almost the same expression he had when she walked off to Drake's room and suddenly Calandra pieces something together.

"You knew this was there didn't you?" She stares over at Jarreth, desperate. "And you let me go over there without a warning or anything?" The realization cuts through her much deeper than she expected.

Jarreth's expression goes blank, he's at a total loss. "What was I supposed to do Cal?" He finally asks.

She's caught off guard. Surely he could have said something. He should have given her some sort of a warning, but would it have lessened the blow at all?

"What does this mean? Why is she in this picture?" She asks, ignoring his question.

Drake returns with a cup and places it in front of Calandra. He looks between Calandra and Jarreth and disappears into his room without a word. *Weird,* Calandra thinks.

"It's— complicated?" Jarreth fights for more to say, but comes up at a loss.

Calandra feels her jaw drop, but she can't

do anything to stop it. It doesn't make any sense, her mom can't have a connection to Jarreth and Drake. She opens her mouth to ask more, but nothing comes out.

Jarreth places his hand on her thigh and shh's her. "I will explain the entire story if you want. You'll need to know it anyways, but you have to tell me that you're ready for it dear."

Calandra scoffs. "I wasn't ready for any of this and yet here I am." She forces a smile and picks up the tea Drake brought her. It's very fruity and burns going down but it takes the edge off of her nerves as the aroma coming off the tea sifts through the air around her. "Go ahead," she says as she slowly sips her drink.

Jarreth takes a deep breath before beginning his explanation. "I told you about humans being banned from Faerie because of an issue between a Fae and a human. What I didn't fully explain before is that the issue was actually a love affair." Calandra nods remembering his earlier mention of the fallout. "The Faerie that caused the issue was the daughter of the ruler at that time, Oberen, he is the original ruler of Faerie. His daughter was your great grandmother, Echo, she fell for one of the humans that spent a lot of time here. Oberen didn't like the thought of mixing bloodlines, especially not in royalty, as he considered himself and his family. Oberen was advised to put an end to the relationship by banning Echo from the world, at least until she came to her senses on things. What Oberen didn't realize when he did this is that Echo was with child. The fact that Oberen was so prejudice against the humans that he would disown his own daughter was his downfall as well as the downfall of our world. I've already told you what happened once the humans were banned."

Calandra downs the rest of her drink as she listens. Jarreth takes the cup from her. "I'll be right back." He assures her before he leaves the room.

Calandra looks around the room and tries to remember the way she felt before she found the picture. She realizes that Drake is standing in the doorway with his arms crossed, listening to the story as well. Surely he knows the story, so why he's so interested in listening makes Calandra wonder. Maybe there's something he wants to be sure Jarreth doesn't disclose. That thought sets her nerves on fire. But Calandra knows how much Jarreth hates Drake, surely he wouldn't be keeping any secrets for Drake. Jarreth returns with a new drink and hands it to her.

"I still don't understand how all of this makes any sense. The story you're giving me has nothing to do with my mother." She tells Jarreth pulling herself away from her thoughts.

"I'm getting to that. After Oberen's fall, the will of the leadership of the world was left hanging in the balance. There were other rulers that came out, most of them did nothing but make matters worse than they already were. The world was off balance, things were getting out of hand, and we needed a solution. Echo never returned to our world, she stayed in the mortal world and decided to live the rest of her life as a mortal. Faeries eventually will loose their power and magic if they stay in the mortal world, they need to draw from Faerie in order to stay strong. Echo gave birth and decided not to tell anyone about her Faerie background. It was at this point that a prophecy was made, a prophecy that someone would be born that would have the ability to put the world back in place. Since the prophecy came shortly after your grandmother was born, it was assumed that she was the one that was predicted. She however, never came to Faerie, even after discovering its existence. She did, however, give birth to a daughter before she passed. Your mother, Hollyn."

"And she was supposed to be the one?" Calandra asks.

"We're not real sure honestly Cal. Everyone of course thought so, including your mother. She took to the prospect of the task willingly and seemed to enjoy her time here and be right at home." Jarreth touches her shoulder where her dragonfly signifies her destiny. "But then she suddenly left, it didn't seem to make any sense."

"Like any of this does." Calandra rolls her eyes.

Jarreth looks away from her and pulls his hand off her shoulder. There's a look on his face that is somewhere between ashamed and embarrassed and Calandra can't make any sense of it. She runs through everything he's just told her again in her head. She sees images in her head as she goes through the gory details of the lies that have made up her life. Suddenly a few details click into place and bring on an even more disturbing realization.

"So, why did she leave? How much of this does my father know?" The words taste acidic as they leave her mouth.

Jarreth doesn't look up at her. Calandra gulps down the last half of her drink at once trying to get the thoughts out of her head. Jarreth grabs the cup from her and returns to the kitchen without saying a word.

Calandra has never exactly had a good relationship with her father, things have always been complicated between the two of them. But never in a million years would she have guessed that their situation existed on this magnitude of complications. Calandra is convinced that her heart isn't beating anymore at all, it can't be after the shock of this revelation.

Lost in her thoughts, Calandra doesn't even hear him enter the room, she has no clue he's there until he is sitting next to her. "What's wrong Cali?" Tristan asks, his voice laced with concern.

Why he would care after the experience they had earlier is beyond her, but his concern is the final straw that breaks her down. Tears flow from her eyes and she leans into him, not caring whether he wants her to or not. Tristan wraps his arms around her and pulls the picture frame out of her hand.

"Is that your mom?" He asks confused.

Calandra nods in agreement without lifting her head from his shoulder. "Everything, my entire life, has been a lie." She knows it can't make any sense or come anywhere close to explaining everything, but it's the only words she can manage to form at the moment.

A cup slams on the table and liquid splashes everywhere. Calandra pulls herself away from Tristan and looks up to see Jarreth standing at the table across from them. His face and eyes are red, and his entire body is stiff as a board. An image of a cartoon character with steam coming out of their ears pops into Calandra's mind.

Incoherent words start to fly between Tristan and Jarreth and Calandra can't even make out who's speaking anymore. Names are shooting out everywhere and she knows before long the fists will probably start coming out as well. Nothing is clear in her head as she watches the scene unfold in front of her. She feels like one of the characters from Peanuts when their parents talk to them, all she can hear is jumbled up nonsense. Everything is too much, she can't even begin to figure out how to deal with this on top of what she's just learned. She finds it hard to believe the guys don't have enough respect for her to behave for just a few moments after everything she's been through.

Calandra feels her breathing go off balance and her ears feel like she's underwater. There's some sort of pressure building inside of her, she can feel it about to boil over, but she's incapable of stopping it. Once it finally hits the top, everything goes silent. Calandra pulls herself to the present scene and looks up wondering what has made them stop. The air gets caught in her throat when she sees what's in front of her.

They are frozen in time it seems. Tristan stands on one side of the table, right next to the couch with his arms in the air, one of them is balled up into a fist. Jarreth is just on the other side of the table, his eyes still red and his entire body tensed up. The cup that she assumes was full of her new tea when it arrived, before Jarreth slammed it onto the table, sits on the table the top third of the liquid is no longer in it and the there is broken glass scattered around it. No one is moving, not even to breathe. Time is somehow standing still.

Calandra reaches over and picks up the cup from the table and sloshes the liquid around before she carefully pours some into her mouth. She continues to look around the room and notices Drake isn't standing in the doorframe like he was the last time she'd seen him. Before she has time to wonder where he went, she feels words on her ear.

"Well well, discovered a new power have we?" Drake is beyond close to her, he places his arms right up against her legs as he leans into her.

She automatically leans away from him and looks at him, confused. *Is that what this is?* she wonders. "Did I make this happen?" She asks.

A devious smile comes over him and he finally stands up and gives Calandra some room. "That you did." He is looking at the frozen scene in front of him with a disturbingly pleased look on his face. "Stopping time is a wonderful gift that many would kill for." He says finally.

"Wait!" Calandra puts the glass back on the table. "If I've frozen time, then why aren't you frozen?" She asks.

Drake laughs menacingly. "This is one of my powers as well dear, which leaves me unaffected by it, as you are."

Oh great, she thinks. A power that could be

somewhat useful, and it's ineffective on the one person she'd like to be able to freeze. This day just keeps on getting better doesn't it? Without saying a word, Calandra heads for the door. She needs away, she needs peace, she needs the field of innocence. Her body is literally aching for it. Just as she reaches for the doorknob, Drake is right next to her again. How did he get here so fast? She wonders.

"Just so you know, I can undo this of course, as can you. But I wouldn't tell Jarreth of your new discovery if I were you."

Calandra almost asks why, but decides it would probably be useless and decides against it.

"Do feel welcome back anytime." Drake runs a finger down her jaw leaving a cold, chilling sensation behind.

And with that Calandra opens the door and runs out and directly to the field of innocence in hopes if finding some sort of comfort there.

Chapter 16
Only Tempts

The wind spins around her, awakening every sense and nerve in her body. She feels alive, on fire, whole. Connecting with the tree in the field the way she had the first time she'd come to draw comfort from it could quickly become her favorite thing to do. Something about it makes her feel right, not to mention much more powerful, which is a feeling she is really beginning to like. The rustle of the leaves fill the air with noise as well as a lovely scent that reminds her of autumn, which conveniently happens to be her favorite season. The power that she received after she was marked with the dragonfly feels so intense at the moment that she feels as if she might explode at any moment.

"And what makes you think I want you here?" She asks without removing her hand from the tree or opening her eyes. How she knew it was Drake approaching without seeing him she was unsure of. Something about the scent in the air changed, it smelled musty with a hint of cedar, and somehow she knew that meant Drake was behind her.

"What makes you think I had your best interests in mind when I decided to show up?" he asks deviously. "Having fun toying with your powers, are we?"

Calandra scoffs and knows she won't be able to keep her concentration up with Drake irritating her. She moves away from the tree and turns to face him. "I'm not toying with anything." She says looking back to the tree and instantly missing the intensity her power had when she was connecting with it.

"You have no clue what you're doing."

Like that wasn't obvious. Calandra is more than aware that she knows nothing of her powers and Jarreth is no help with it. Every time she brings up wanting to work on them, he just changes the subject. Tristan of course wants nothing to do with any of it. She knows that surely she has some abilities she hasn't used or discovered yet. She can feel in her bones that there has to be more there that isn't being touched. She has a desire to tap into them and discover what all she can do. A desire that Jarreth apparently wants to remain hidden and Tristan wants to pretend doesn't exist at all.

"Where's Jarreth?" Calandra asks wondering why he's not the one that came after her. Was he really that mad that she had challenged him for once.

Drake rolls his eyes. "He figured you could

use some time alone."

"So that's why you're here?"

"I didn't agree with him. Plus I wanted to take advantage of some time with you without Jarreth around for once." Drake arches an eyebrow, which turns his statement into some sort of a dare.

Calandra rolls her eyes.

"Don't get an attitude Calandra, I can help you." His smile turns dangerous and sends a cold shiver through Calandra.

"Help me with what exactly?"

Calandra didn't realize he had moved, but he is suddenly right next to her, his words touch her skin before she hears them. "With your powers," he whispers, "I know you want to figure them out and I'm willing to bet Jarreth doesn't want to show you how."

As soon as he says it, there are multiple small faeries flying into the field. They are all blue, purple, green, or pink, and they are glowing. There is a ring of light matching their color surrounding them. They aren't much larger than a dragonfly. They have long flowing hair and sunken in eyes. Calandra watches in amazement as they aimlessly grace the field in flight and the fluttering of their wings fills the air.

"Sprites," Drake whispers into her ear again. "Here for— demonstration purposes." Before Calandra can question it, Drake starts in on another explanation. "Do it again."

"What?" She asks and wonders why she sounds so breathless.

"Stop time, like you did earlier."

"I'd have to know how I did it in order for that to work," she scoffs.

"Focus!"

"On what exactly?"

"Your surroundings," he responds, "listen to it, listen to nature. Use that power, like you were doing when I got here. But this time, channel it and make it do what you want it to."

Calandra closes her eyes and focuses on the field around her. She hears the leaves rustle in the soft breeze that blows around them. She takes in the soft forest smell. The wood scent is mixed with musk and cedar now that Drake is here. The soft flutter of sprite wings surrounds them. She lets the sounds and the smells fill her and allows the peace and comfort of the beauty of nature to take control of her. She feels the sparks of power start to fill her and it leaves her with a desire to do something with it. Now she just has to figure out how to. Focus, she tells herself. She takes a deep breath and centers herself onto the power that fills her. Without any control of it, her arm lifts slightly in the air and she feels the power pulse through and out of it.

Drake sucks in a breath of air which lets Calandra know she's done it before she opens her eyes to verify. Sure enough, the sounds have stopped, the field is completely still and silent. Too silent, it's an eerie send chills straight to your soul kind of quiet. The sprites are all frozen in the air, their wings have stopped mid-flight. Calandra gasps at the sight. Something deep down tells her to feel mortified at what she's done. These are creatures; living, breathing beings, that are now stilled in mid-air, because of her. Surely this is a new low for her. But in actuality, all she feels is powerful. A new sense of accomplishment spreads over her.

"There now, that wasn't so hard was it?" His voice is still in her ear, tickling her skin.

She nods, finding herself somehow unable to speak and more than slightly short of breath. Before she can object, she feels his hands on her shoulders. A chill goes through her. "Now I want you to try something else." He explains. "Close your eyes and picture a storm."

Calandra opens her mouth to ask a question, but he shushes her before anything comes out.

"Just focus." Drake's hands begin to move back and forth on her shoulders. She feels power radiating off of him and seeping into her. "Picture a storm, thunder and lightning. Hear it in your mind, pull from the power in you, and focus."

Calandra takes another deep calming breath. She pictures a thunderstorm in her mind. She imagines storm clouds rolling into the field and bringing the sounds of nature's fury with it.

She envisions lightning accompanying the rolling thunder. The smell of rain ensures her that she is using the power the way she's been instructed to do so.

"The thunder rolls," she feels and hears Drake's words in her ear. She opens her eyes and sees that everything she's been envisioning surrounds them. The field is dark with gray storm clouds. The visual she had in her head has been replicated here in real life. The thunder softly booms around them and shortly after it, lightning rolls under the clouds above.

A sense of accomplishment washes over her in knowing that she made this happen. She controlled nature and made it do what she desired. Her heart is racing along with the feeling coursing through her from the chill Drake has started in her. The blending of sensations sends her on a whole new sense of Euphoria.

"Euphoria." She says without meaning to. Calandra closes her eyes, relishing in all the new sensations that are coursing through her.

Guilt courses through her as the reality of

what she's done settles on her. She wonders what came over her exactly and why she allowed herself to take advantage of the Sprites all so she could get a tiny moment of accomplishment. "I shouldn't have done that," she whispers.

"Ah ah ah!" Drake scolds her. "Evil never judges dear Calandra, it only tempts. Don't let yourself overthink it dear, just relish in the joy of it all."

She opens her eyes and isn't entirely surprised to find Drake has disappeared altogether. She wills time to move again and the sprites all shoot her an evil glance, call her names, and dart away angrily. The storm clouds slowly roll away and take the sounds of nature's accusing fury with them. Calandra lies down in the grass, spreads her legs out, and covers her face with her arms to hide her eyes from the beauty around her that she doesn't deserve at the moment.

LAINY LANE

Chapter 17
Right & Wrong

A rustle in the brush on the edge of the field pulls Calandra from her daze that is on the verge of becoming a slumber, even though she's pretty sure she's only been lying there for a few minutes at the most. She sits up instantly and looks around trying to see where the noise came from. Her fear at the moment is that the sprites are back for revenge. Instead she notices two figures standing in the trees, but they are much too large to be sprites.

"Who's there?" She calls in the direction of the noise.

Her heart drops into her feet when she sees Tristan and Jarreth walk out of the trees and head towards her, both of their expressions are unreadable. Her breath catches in her throat as she wonders how long they've been there. However, the look on Tristan's face once they get closer answers that question for her. He is hurt—again. *Great*. She rolls her eyes at herself for the situation she has managed to get herself into. Somehow Jarreth doesn't look hurt, or mad, or upset at all, which leaves Calandra feeling lost and confused.

She can feel the fire radiating off of Tristan and his speed increases the closer they get to her. Actually, that isn't heat, that's fury. Why is she feeling that?

"So— " The word falls out of her mouth when they finally reach her, and she immediately wishes she could suck it back up.

"So," Tristan begins, his entire face is red. "What exactly is this destiny you have to stay here to fill, do everything wrong and disregard everything that you know about being a decent human being?"

"I— wow!" Calandra's brain can't seem to form any sort of response. She didn't expect him to be this mad, he's not usually the type of person to loose his cool and be mean to her, and she is more than a little thrown off by it.

"Tristan," Jarreth warns. He's standing right next to Calandra, looking slightly timid but not mad at all. So maybe she hasn't messed up everything, which would be nice.

"Don't start with me!" Tristan yells and points his finger at Jarreth. "You're the one who started this in the first place!"

"Tristan!" Calandra shrieks.

"Don't!" He turns his attention back to Calandra. "Just don't!" Tristan puts his head in his hands and starts to pace.

Calandra looks over to Jarreth, lost. Jarreth

simply shrugs and looks away from her. So he is upset too, just not to the same extent that Tristan is. Calandra takes a deep breath, resolving to herself that she got herself into this situation so it's going to be up to her to get herself out of it—somehow. She walks over to Tristan slowly and reaches up for him, he pulls away instantly and glares at her.

Then something from her earlier experience with Drake comes into her mind. *Will the power to do what you want it to.* She had just willed her power to make a storm roll in earlier, and now she is feeling Tristan's emotions for some reason. Does that mean she can will her power to change those emotions? She still doesn't know exactly what she is doing, but after the ordeal with Drake she now has a better idea now of how to use her powers, so she figures it has to be worth a shot. It's probably the only shot she is going to get for now. It's an easy way out, so she opts to take it.

Calandra focuses on the feelings radiating off of Tristan. The hurt, anger, and deception. She lets them fill her. Her heart breaks all on it's own when it occurs to her that Tristan is feeling these emotions so immensely because of her. She falters for a minute realizing that what she's about to do is beyond wrong. It is an invasion of privacy. She turns to look at Jarreth, trying to make up her mind on what she should do. He shrugs and nudges his head towards Tristan. When Calandra turns back to Tristan, the glare he gives her finally settles her mind.

She focuses on his feelings again, being extra careful to not let them reach her conscience this time. Before it has time to overload her senses, she refocuses on the power inside her. Without as much effort as the previous attempts had taken, she is able to will the power to do exactly as she wants it to. Tristan's expression goes blank for a minute and then he's back. He is the normal and once again unhurt Tristan. His anger is gone and Calandra's nerves ease up as she realizes he isn't mad at her any longer.

He looks back and forth between Jarreth and Calandra. "I guess I should get back to

Drake's. I don't think I'm supposed to be here."

It isn't until Tristan speaks and clarifies that she has been successful that she realizes she has once again done exactly what Tristan said she would. She knew that messing with his emotions and using her powers to change them was wrong. She knew that it went against everything she had ever been taught. Knowing all of that hadn't stopped her from doing it.

Calandra looks back to Jarreth, afraid of what he may be thinking of her. Surprisingly, he looks rather impressed. She isn't impressed with herself in the least, she is more than disgusted with her behavior today.

"Thanks for coming to check on me." She tells Tristan, unsure of what else to say, or what he will remember about how and why he is here.

"You are ok, right?" Tristan asks, sincerely concerned.

Calandra nods and gives a small smile as her heart twitches in her chest.

"Ok then," Tristan awkwardly looks at Jarreth again and walks away.

Jarreth waits until Tristan is completely out of earshot before he brings up the obvious.

"No, he doesn't remember any of it," he tells her. "It's as if it never happened."

"It's that easy?" She asks and the question surprises her.

Jarreth doesn't respond, so Calandra turns around to look at him. He looks sad and concerned.

"Trust me, I won't be doing it again!" She blurts out, each word spills over the next.

Jarreth smiles, it's a very small smile, but still beyond comforting in the current situation.

"And I'd never try it on you." She isn't sure why she says it, the words are out before she realizes it.

"You could try all you wanted to." He smiles and taps her nose. "But it wouldn't work on me."

Calandra sighs and takes a seat in the grass. She places her hands on the ground next to her and takes comfort from the field.

"Guess I messed things up— again." She says when Jarreth takes a seat in front of her.

"I must say I am impressed."

"What? That I can turn evil and deceive people?" Calandra scoffs.

"Calandra, you are part faerie. I already explained to you the line between good and evil is blurred for Fae. After seeing the way you've already developed so many powers and learned to control them, I'm really starting to wonder just how much Fae you have in you."

Calandra looks at him confused. "But my mom was part human right?"

"Yes," he replies, "that is the story. But you are doing things you shouldn't be able to do for someone who is only part Fae, let alone someone who hasn't had time to develop her powers yet. Something is— different about you."

"Different?" Calandra shows her offense in her voice.

Jarreth chuckles. "Special."

She smiles at the new direction he's taken. "Thanks, I guess. I'm sorry for— well all of it."

Jarreth places his hand on top of hers. "Calandra, I need to be sure you truly understand what I told you before. About who you love directly effecting the types of powers you have and the outcome of this world." He sighs as he looks at her, concern clear in his eyes.

"I believe you." She says as she thinks back to their conversation at the bar.

"What you did here today, not only with Drake, but what you did to Tristan when he left—that's the kind of thing I was talking about Calandra. Hanging around with dark people is going to make you do dark things, whether you believe it will or not. With all seriousness, you have the ability to make or break this world. Whether you want it or not, it's entirely in your hands."

She blushes, ashamed of herself. "It's just that I was so excited to try and learn how to use my powers that I couldn't say no when Drake offered to help me. As far as the stopping time at his house, well I didn't mean to do that." She remembers as soon as the words slip out that she wasn't supposed to say anything about the last part.

Jarreth's face blanks out for a moment. "You stopped time at Drake's house?"

She nods slightly.

He stares at her blankly for a few very uncomfortable moments. "Wow!" He finally says under his breath.

"I didn't even know how I did it. I was stressed out with you and Tristan arguing and the next thing I knew, Drake and I were the only ones still moving." She shrugs as if it was no big deal. To her, it hadn't seemed like that big of a deal, she'd done it on accident and hadn't meant any harm by it. Honestly, it was probably the only thing that had kept them from a fistfight, so in actuality, she had probably done everyone some good. "How did you not know I did it? I mean, what happened after I left and things— you know, started again?"

Jarreth smirks, "I guess Drake took the wrap for you. He said that he did it to give you a minute and that you had been so upset that you said you wanted to be alone, so he gave you a head start. I didn't trust him to actually leave you alone. I was halfway here before I realized Tristan was following me. Sorry I guess I kind of caused more drama between you two."

Calandra laughs, though she's not totally sure why. "You didn't cause it, I did." She looks down at the ground and picks at the grass. "Why weren't you guys affected by the time being stopped here? How did you see what happened?"

"We arrived after you had already stopped things, so we weren't effected by it. This is why I wanted you to learn about powers before you go using them," he says it matter-of-factly.

"Oh," Calandra sighs and blushes slightly.

"Have you ever been to a Masquerade Ball?" Jarreth throws the question out randomly, bringing Calandra out of her moping.

She looks up at him questioningly, "no."

He smiles, "it's an old tradition really. Masks are kind of a big thing with Fae, it's the mystery of it and also the ability to deceive, of course." His smile broadens, "Drake does a ball every year."

"A ball of the masquerade kind?" Calandra

laughs as she watches Jarreth unsure of where this is leading to exactly.

"Yes, that's the kind. It's in two weeks."

"Hmm," she smiles.

"As it turns out, I have a dress of your great grandmothers, a dress that Echo had made specifically for her. Your mother always admired it and wanted to find a chance to wear it. I do believe it happens to be just your size."

"Must be the genes," Calandra jokes.

"Either way, I figured you might want to wear it to the ball." He smiles confidently at her.

Calandra's heart swells to what feels like should be far beyond her chest cavity. A dress that is part of her family heritage. A dress that was something her mother wanted. A piece of the people that have made her into what she is, the people she never had a chance to meet. The thoughts flow through her head and fill her with excitement at the magical possibilities of it all. It's a chance she never would have come across in a million years in the mortal world with her dad.

"Of course I would," she finally says when

she realizes that Jarreth is still looking at her anticipating a response.

"Then it's yours," he smiles, "I can escort you to the ball as well if you'd like. I have a feeling Drake isn't going to allow Tristan to come."

"I have a feeling he wouldn't want to go with me regardless."

Jarreth shakes his head in disagreement, "I think you underestimate that boys love for you dear."

Calandra shrugs, unsure of what to think of that statement.

LAINY LANE

Chapter 18
Masquerade

Calandra stands in the room, looking at herself in the mirror, in awe and completely and utterly dazed. The dress Jarreth gave her of Echo's was amazingly beautiful, but she feels completely out of place in it. She doesn't belong in something like this, she isn't meant to look this glamorous. The dress is an iridescent silver color. The top is a beautiful corset that silhouettes her figure and drapes around her hips before coming to a V-shape in the front and the back. This dress shows her off in a way that she's never done before. A way that makes her feel beyond self-conscious. Nothing is revealed, but she's never dressed to impress, so to speak, before and the thought that this outfit will be drawing eyes to her has her nerves set on fire. The corset is intricately embroidered with a blue thread that matches the color of Jarreth's eyes. The skirt consists of layers upon layers of ruffled tulle and it swishes as she moves.

    Her mask is laying on the bed still, she walks over to it, unable to look at the mirror any longer. She can't seem to recognize the girl that stares back at her. The mask is the perfect compliment to her dress, she figures it has to have been made just for it. It is the exact same shade of silver and framed with jewels. The top has one blue jewel that matches the embroidery in the dress and the remainder of the jewels that make up the frame of the mask are a mixture of light blues, silver, and clear. The gems peak at the top of the mask, just above the large blue gem. There is a small strand of silver beads that hang run below the large blue stone and frame just above the eyebrows in a swirl fashion. On the right corner of the mask is a beautiful baby blue flower with a few silver tulle petals and silver flowers resting above and below it.

She grabs the mask and holds it over her face and turns back to the mirror. She freezes and her breath catches when she sees the image looking back at her. Who is that? She wonders to herself. This is not an image she's ever seen in the mirror before. This girl is stunning, mysterious, and confident. All of which are things that Calandra has never felt in herself before. Her hair is done up in spiral curls and full of body with little flowers and streamers holding the top half back and out of her face. She is so caught up in the picture in front of her that she doesn't hear Jarreth come into the room. He stands at the door and stares at her for a few minutes before he finally makes his way into the room.

He walks up behind her and places his arm around her shoulders, "you're breathtaking!"

Calandra breaks out of her trance and looks at his reflection standing behind her in the mirror and she smiles.

Jarreth is wearing an all white suit with a light blue tie. There are eloquently placed sequins throughout the suit that catch the light just right and in all the right places to magnify his beauty. He uses his arm around her to spin her around and make her face him. "There is one thing that I think I failed to mention about the ball that I should probably warn you of."

Her face turns grim and fear courses through her. The last couple of weeks had been going great, more than great. Her and Jarreth had been getting to know each other and she began feeling even more connected to the world as well. She was finally starting to feel confident in her ability to be able to fulfill her destiny. Could what he was about to tell her possibly ruin all of that? Jarreth pulls her over to the bed and sits down next to her, his hand remains on her shoulder which sends the comforting sparks through her, it is a sensation that she is beginning to think she will never get totally used to.

"I told you humans were banned from our world at the fallout," Jarreth begins his explanation and sends Calandra's heart into overdrive. She nods remembering the story he had told her weeks ago. "There was one little piece of information that I left out."

Her heart drops. "Wait just a minute," she tells him, her breath slows to an almost dormant pace. She ponders to herself if she really wants this revelation or not. "Is this something I absolutely have to know beforehand?" she asks finally.

Jarreth nods.

Calandra takes a deep breath, "ok then do something for me first, just in case." She smiles slightly and holds her hand out towards him, not bothering to explain her request or wait for a response.

He eyes her cautiously and gives her an odd look before he gives into her request. He closes his eyes and instantly her anxiety and fear about what he is about to say melts away completely. Calandra sighs in the relief of their absence.

"Better?"

She smiles innocently, "I just want to be on an open emotional field in case things get totally discombobulated after whatever it is you have to say."

Jarreth sighs, "basically, with no human interaction at all to feed certain— needs," Jarreth stumbles to find the word to use, "most Fae would die out completely. So, after the fallout, we had to find a way to control things. There had to be a balance, so that there wouldn't be enough interaction for things to get out of hand as they once had. But we still needed enough to keep things in tact here as well." Jarreth picks up her hand and brushes his fingers against her knuckles, washing away the spikes of nerves that shoot through her as he speaks. "Which is why Drake decided to host a Masquerade ball every year. It's the one night that we're allowed to have humans come in. It may sound cruel, but it's really the only way for us to survive."

A statement that Calandra had heard said in a sermon once runs through her mind, *"Don't hate the person, hate the sin in the person."* Calandra knows somewhere deep down she should probably be completely disturbed by this. After the last several weeks that she's been here and given the things she's seen and learned, this doesn't really seem too bad in retrospect. She must be softening up to the things that would have disturbed her at one point.

She wonders when that change began as she can't recall consciously deciding to allow that to happen. She still hasn't learned about all of the hungers and needs of the different Fae here, but she knows they are there and that they differ for each type of faerie. She has learned some of the different needs. Others, much like a lot of things, Jarreth doesn't want to explain to her. Faeries are very emotional creatures, so the thought of what she may see tonight does send chills through her, but she knows she must accept all aspects of this world and it's people. As she sees to be the way of life, she has to give this world a chance before she is able to come up with any sort of opinion for it.

"Ok," she replies simply.

"Ok?" Jarreth seems to be taken aback by the simplicity of her response.

She nods.

"Ok—" He seems reluctant still but decides not to question her decision any further, "ready to go then?"

She nods and stands. Jarreth stands and holds out a bended elbow to escort her. She loops her arm into his, smiles, and lets him lead her into the mysterious night. A night that she no longer knows what to expect from, in the body of a remarkably beautiful and confidant woman that she isn't sure she knows.

****

What Calandra wasn't at all prepared for was where the ball was going to be. Why Jarreth hadn't mentioned that the field the venue of choice was beyond her. It is a more than breathtaking scene. The tree that she has connected with several times is surrounded in gleaming lights and it looks simply magnificent. There are lines of lights forming a sort of canopy ceiling above the entire field, though they are not laced together on a string, instead each individual light is suspended in the air all on its own. Just to the right of the large tree that Calandra favors, are three large fabric panels that are running through an assortment of colors. To the left of the tree are several large tables holding an assortment of foods and drinks. Calandra notices one table holds nothing but small glasses containing liquid like what Jarreth always drinks, but there is a large variety of colors.

Throughout the field new flowers have popped up. Some look like tulips, some like roses, and others like lilies. However every flower is a rainbow of colors. Despite the elegance of the transformation the field has made from a wonderment of nature to an equally amazing masquerade, the dresses and masks are what really stand out. Everyone looks amazing, humans and Fae alike are all dressed in intricate ballroom dresses and suits with masks to accompany in the mystery of the event. Most of the Fae women, however, have chosen not to wear masks. Instead, they have done fantastical things with their makeup to hide their faces. Makeup not only covers their eyelids, but makes beautiful patterns across their entire faces accompanied with beautifully placed gems, jewels, and glittered pieces of art. Suddenly, the breathtaking and confident creature that Calandra felt when she looked at herself in the mirror before she arrived, seems much more ordinary in comparison.

Jarreth stands behind her and takes her mask out of her hand. He holds it up to his face and breathes on the inside of it and then places it over Calandra's face. She is completely lost as to what the purpose of his gesture was until she realizes that it is staying on without any sort of strings to keep it in place. He does the same to his own mask. Calandra hadn't paid any attention to his mask until now. It is white just as his suit is, but it doesn't cover both of his eyes like most of the masks do. It goes straight across his forehead and on the right side comes down to just above his mouth. But from there it cuts upwards to cover only part of his nose and arches just over his left eye, leaving it fully exposed. It is framed in sequins that are cobalt blue and around the right eye is a swirled pattern of baby blue. It compliments his suit and the beauty that his eyes hold perfectly.

Calandra's stomach does a few catapults when she feels him sweep her from the edge of the field and into the center where everyone is dancing. He spins her around and the beauty of the people and the masks spin in and out of her view. The entire experience is intoxicating. Her body rages with the electric current that comes from his touch. Her eyes are filled with the mystification of the people swirling around her, and to her surprise, they all look equally influenced.

After several euphoric moments of twirling in the breathtaking scene, Jarreth escorts her off of the dance floor and over to the table containing the refreshments for the night. He grabs his go-to pink drink and holds his hand in front of the tables, signaling for Calandra to help herself to something. Her attention remains on the table he has just chosen from. She looks from one side of the shots of liquid to the other, the entire rainbow spectrum is represented. She has only ever had Jarreth's pink concoction. As she has no clue what any of them are, she figures there is no harm in trying out a new color to see what happens. Her conscience immediately flashes to the night a while back when she had convinced him, or rather tricked him, into let her have some of the drink and how that action had ended. She quickly shakes her head free of the memory and goes back to her game of eenie meeney miney moe to pick one out. She subconsciously lands on a purple shot and she takes it down quickly. It is bitter and sends her throat into odd spasms.

Jarreth arches an eyebrow at her response and then smiles.

"You're still not going to tell me what they are?"

"Obviously not knowing isn't stopping you from consuming."

She shrugs and walks over to the next table that has tall glasses filled with different colored smoothies. She grabs one with strawberries on top and begins sipping on it instead of getting another shot of the mystery liquid.

"You never read anything on Faerie folklore, did you?" His question takes her off guard.

She shakes her head and shrugs, "I guess not. Would I have learned anything useful?"

Jarreth shrugs, "probably not too much, though you might think a bit harder before trying drinks and food while you're here. Especially when no one wants to tell you what they are," he chuckles.

His statement sends her back to her first day here. During the awkward walk through the woods to Jarreth's cabin, he had explained to her what he fed on; emotions. He had taken hers away from her but said he didn't use them, that he had simply taken them from her in an effort to help her feel more comfortable. He said on that first day that he had other ways of satisfying his needs. She had been so caught up in too many things at the time to even think to question it. Her eyes grow wide and she turns back to the table filled with the shots. Scenes flash before her eyes of every time she's seen Jarreth's eyes flash different colors. She has seen them turn every single one of the colors that are represented on the table at some point.

"Jarreth?" She turns to face him, "why do your eyes change colors sometimes?"

"It's a Fae trait. It's kind of like a mood ring, it shows our emotions. Young faeries eyes will stay whatever color their mood is. As we get older, we learn to control it and to be able to change them back to our actual color. But we can never keep them from showing it, at least momentarily." He is watching the crowd dance across the dance floor, completely oblivious to the road Calandra is on and where her mind is taking her.

Her heart shatters as the realization hits

her and takes her breath along with it. The colors are emotions. The shots are his way of feeding in the absence of humans. She gulps the rest of her drink down and slams the empty glass back on the table. She quickly grabs another and begins to walk away from the table, unable to be around Jarreth at the moment.

After two steps, Jarreth grabs her arm and spins her around and brings her back to him. "What?" He asks, his voice sincerely confused.

"You let me take that— whatever emotion it is and didn't even tell me!" Her voice is louder than she'd meant for it to be and a few people stop dancing and turn to stare at them.

Jarreth clears his throat and walks them further away from the crowd. "I told you that drinking stuff when you didn't know what it was wasn't the brightest of ideas, you still drank it. And need I remind you that both times you've drank them, you did it all on your own? Don't act like I forced it down your throat!" He informs her.

"Don't give me that Jarreth! You know that had you told me I never would've drank it!" She tries to pull free of him and head back into the crowd, but his grip tightens around her arm. "Let go of me! I don't even want to look at you right now!" She spits the words out and laces them with more hate than what is probably necessary.

It gets her point across as his eyes flash light purple and his face goes blank. His mouth opens to say something and immediately closes again. He drops his arm from her and she storms off into the crowd. She has no clue where she's going, especially since she is already in her favorite place to go when she needs comfort, but getting away from Jarreth is her top priority. Faces keep turning towards her as she makes her way through the dancing bodies surrounding her. Everyone is twisting, turning, swirling, and Calandra is no longer sure if she is walking across the crowd or going in circles along with them.

Her mind is clouding over in confusion when she feels a hand on her back and a familiar chill goes through her body. She doesn't have to turn to know it is Drake touching her. He is wearing all black, as usual, though some of the sequins on his coat seem to be giving off a midnight blue shine. His mask is all black and it has a long nose that slopes down and comes to a point just below his mouth. She can see the corners of his mouth curl up into a smile as he pulls her into him.

"Dance," he says simply. It is a statement, not a question, and his voice is laced with temptation.

She doesn't respond, but she also decides not to fight him either. She's away from Jarreth, and if he by chance decides to come after her and sees her dancing with Drake, it will be a nice bonus thrown in to increase his irritation. She goes along with the twirling movement Drake takes her into, feeling the music pulsing through her harder now that the odd chill from Drake's touch pulses through her with it.

"Where have you been hiding the past couple weeks?" he breaks their silence.

"I haven't been hiding."

"Well I haven't seen you around, not even here. I looked for you a few times. I wanted to be sure you were coming tonight." He winks as he says it.

"You know where you could have found me if you had really wanted to."

"Eh," he scoffs, "I did want to find you, but had no desire to see Jarreth. I Had to pick my battles."

Calandra rolls her eyes.

Something seems different about Drake tonight. He's not quite as snide as he usually is, he seems to actually be somewhat sincere for once. He is giving off a vibe of something that Calandra has never felt from him before, but she's having trouble placing it. She looks at him, watching his eyes for any sign of changes, but is left with nothing. Desire...Is that what it is? Maybe, but desire for what exactly?

"You know—" Drake leans in and whispers in her ear, "if your little argument hasn't ended before the party is over, my invitation is still out there."

And there's Drake, the one Calandra is used to, he's come full circle for her.

"No thanks!"

Luckily the song ends and she turns away from him without another word. She is hoping for an escape to the other side of the crowd like she had originally set out for. But she instead ends up face to face with Tristan.

LAINY LANE

Chapter 19
Mystery

"So, do you wanna talk about what happened in the field a couple weeks ago?" Tristan asks as he takes her in his arms and begins circling her through the crowd again.

Calandra hasn't seen him since the day in the field when she had taken his anger for her away from him. If she was to be totally honest, she had been avoiding him, but she hadn't fully admitted that to herself yet. Tristan is wearing a normal black and white suit. It is not very Masquerade looking, especially compared to everyone else. His mask is a plain black mask on a stick. He certainly doesn't look like he had much time to prepare for the night. But he still looks like Tristan, which is oddly comforting for her.

Calandra looks at him confused, he isn't supposed to remember what happened at the field. She had taken his emotions, and in turn, his memory of the events away. Jarreth said he wouldn't remember it and he certainly seemed to lack the memory when he left the field that day.

Tristan frowns at her lack of response, "Drake told me."

Of course he did. She thinks and rolls her eyes to herself. She should have known better than to think Drake would keep quiet about what happened. Knowing him, he has probably told the entire world about it. She knew better, technically, but somehow at that particular moment all sense had failed her.

"I just— I wanted you to—" Words fail to come to her, at least any that can explain away what she did.

"Don't Cal, just don't!" Oddly enough, he doesn't look mad. He is calm and collected, more so than she's seen him since their arrival here.

"I'm sorry," she settles for a simple apology, it's really the only thing that seems even slightly appropriate.

"Tell me something Cali."

"What?" Her nerves peak as she wonders what he may want to know. She pulls from her powers to calm herself.

"Do you even know who you are anymore?"

Calandra is entirely offended. After what she did to him, she probably doesn't have the right to be offended, but that's exactly what she finds herself feeling. "I will not respond to that!" she scoffs.

"Really?"

"Really. Look, I'm sorry for what I did, I regret it greatly. But that doesn't give you the right to act like this Tristan."

"I think I have every right after everything," the attitude returns to Tristan's voice.

"To be upset, yes. To be flat out rude to me, no."

Tristan sighs, "look, I'm just trying to understand all of this Calandra. So much has changed, about you, about us. I just don't get it. This isn't you. This isn't my Cali. My Cali is a good sweet girl that knows the difference between right and wrong and always puts others before herself."

"I'm sorry." She realizes that she has said that every time she's seen Tristan since their arrival and she feels stupid for it. Surely there has to be more she can say.

"Do you remember the kiss in the rain, outside of my car at your house?" Tristan smiles as he recalls the memory from several months back, before things had gotten complicated with another world, and back when Tristan was the center of her universe. "You had always wanted to have a romantic kiss in the rain like couples do in the movies, you said. So, when we got to your house and it started raining, I took the chance to fill that for you. But it was so awkward to have all the rain sloshing over us. We were cold, and all we could do was laugh. It may not have been the blockbuster romantic event you'd hoped for exactly, but it was one of the greatest nights I've ever had because it was genuine."

"Tristan don't—" she puts her hand over his mouth to stop him from continuing the story.

"Talk to me Calandra, please." He looks desperate, he is begging and pleading with his eyes, so she gives in. She takes her mask off and holds it to her side.

"I'm fragile right now is all, in a bit of a damaged state." The pain is clear in her eyes and Calandra takes a deep breath to push it away quickly. She feels powerful and resolved with the mask of blank emotions pulled back over her face, which is quite fitting at a masquerade ball.

"I guess you don't even need that thing at all, do you?" Tristan points to the actual masquerade mask in her hand by her side. "Your powers give you a mask of your own apparently." Feelings flash across Tristan's face one by one;

hurt, betrayal, confusion, and desperation. Calandra finds herself wondering what colors his eyes would flash for those emotions if he were Fae.

"Don't—" Calandra replies simply, breathing harder to ensure her true emotions don't come through.

"What Cal? Don't make you feel what you actually feel? Don't remind you of who you really are? Don't tell you what you actually believe? What you know deep down in your heart to be true? Don't tell you that you're ignoring every moral that your father worked so hard to instill in you? The morals that you used to know how to stand up for." Every emotion but irritation drains from him immediately.

"I just can't deal with my past right now Tristan, I need to focus on my future. I need to focus on me for once." The excuse even has her fooled, at least momentarily. She is taken aback at how easily she came up with it. It flows out of her mouth naturally, maybe a bit too naturally. Calandra looks away from him, pulls her gaze to the ground, ashamed, and looks back at him once she's sure the emotion is gone.

Tristan unexpectedly pulls her to him with a desperate force behind it. She buries her head into him and nuzzles into his neck, doing her best to keep it together. It's so easy to fall to pieces with Tristan, he knows exactly what to do when she needs it, but that's not who she is anymore.

"You know that your past influences your future no matter how hard you try to fight it. What you know to be true will never fully leave you Calandra, even if you try and force it to. The truth can't suddenly become untrue." Tristan whispers into her neck, the words touch her neck and she feels them against her skin before they register in her mind.

"You know that I love you Tristan," Calandra says softly, lifting her head and gazing off into the distance somewhere.

Tristan knows where this is going. He knows exactly why she's suddenly confirming her feelings for him. She's gone again and the rejection is coming once more. He takes in her scent again before he pulls away from her, readying himself for what is to come.

"I just can't do this." A tear threatens to fall and she quickly wipes it away before it has a chance.

"I miss you. I miss my Cali, and if she ever decides to come back, please let me know." Tristan's voice is intense, more so than Calandra's ever heard it before.

"I'm right here," Calandra replies simply.

"No, you're not, you slipped away, long ago. The moment that it happened is etched into my memory forever and, at this point, I'm not sure you'll ever be back again. And nothing will ever be the same because of it."

Calandra starts to say something but stops herself. She is afraid of how much her comment would reveal, so she swallows it down instead. She stares at him in bewilderment and wonders how they managed to get to this point.

Tristan's light touch is on her shoulder, tracing her mark and sending a shiver through her. "One side is blue and the other is purple."

Calandra looks down at it and realizes she's never noticed the contrast of the swirls in the wings. It's like a ying yang with one side baby blue, the other lavender. She looks into the crowd and sees them off in the distance, standing on the same sides as they are represented in the mark. Jarreth is to the left and has his mask with baby blue swirls hanging at his side. Drake is on the right and his lavender eyes smolder into her. Calandra brings her gaze back to Tristan who still stands in front of her waiting for her to piece his meaning together. And in that moment she realizes, there is no color to represent Tristan. He's not a part of this and the truth that she's been keeping buried deep down inside of her, unwilling to deal with, comes up suddenly. The tear escapes finally while she stares at Tristan and this time she doesn't stop it.

Tristan watches it trail down her face and knows she's finally put two and two together in her mind and he can feel the loss that it leaves him in. He puts his plain black mask back on to cover his own emotions and uses his gloved hand to wipe the tear from of her face. "You can't have one without the other, just like light can't exist without the dark. One day you'll understand that."

"Don't leave—" the words are barely audible as she fights to keep them from escaping.

"You know I'll always be here for you." Tristan looks at the ground as he says it. Then his gaze comes up through the mask, though his head doesn't move from the ground. "But I'm part of the past that you can't deal with tonight. This," Tristan motions around him at the masquerade scene that surrounds them, "is the future you are focusing on and I'm not part of it, so I guess I'll leave you to it." He leans into her, one gloved hand on her cheek and places a quick kiss on her other cheek. He catches the new tear tracking down her face in the process. "I'll be— around, should you ever decide to go back to your roots again." With that, he turns and walks away.

Her body tries to pull toward him. There is a gravity that is telling her to go after him, but with one quick breath she fights it down. Another breath brings in enough power to bring her emotions back under control. She pulls her masquerade mask back to her face and walks over to them. She stands in between her ying yang. Jarreth to one side, Drake to the other. Their masks are in place as well as they watch the ball unfold around them. Calandra takes one more look at her shoulder, and realizes that she is the body of the dragonfly while they are the wings.

The realization stuns her and leaves her hungry for Tristan's place in it all. *I'll always need him.* The words fill her head and she does her best to fight them back down. Jarreth reaches his arm out to her inviting her for a dance, which is just the spell she needs to clear her mind and emotions. His eyes flash a cobalt blue before returning to baby blue. She turns and steals a glance at Drake, green crosses into his eyes before they fade back to lavender. She smiles wickedly as she turns back around and takes Jarreth's hand, letting him lead her to the dance floor and losing herself in the bodies that swirl around them. Just like that, she's forgotten about the good and bad and old beliefs talk from Tristan and given into what's around her instead.

Tristan waits just outside of the field, hoping she is still coming after him. He believes that some part of what they used to share can fight through her newfound love of power and desires and that she'll rush out to fix what has become of them. He knows that she has to know what is right and wrong. She has to know that she is falling into sin and temptation, all of the things that she's been warned to stay away from. Even if she's in another world, the same rules still apply. He resolves to do whatever it takes to remind her of the values and the God that she once dedicated her life to faithfully. After several minutes, he sighs, realizing he has indeed truly lost her completely and he leaves with a new level of hurt going through him.

Jarreth returns her to the concession table after their dance. Their fight has been completely forgotten. Calandra can't remember exactly when she had decided to forgive him, but somewhere on the dance floor she found herself no longer mad or upset at all.

A strange mask catches her eye out on the dance floor. He is a tall, sturdy man and dressed in an all black suit with a matte finish. His hair is messily thrown about and a familiar shade of copper. His mask is what really sets him apart from the other people that crowd the field tonight. The mask is black, with eight points that come up over his head. The points make out what look like antlers that range in size. The longest ones are on the outside and the shortest on the inside. The eyeholes are not the same oblong shape as the other masks, instead they are squared on one side. The bottom of the mask has two more points that come down and cross over each other to make an X just under his mouth.

He is staring directly at Calandra and Jarreth. Between the shadow of his mask and the shadows of being in the dimly lit field at night, Calandra can't make out his eyes. But even without seeing them, she can sense that he is staring into her and Jarreth. Something is vaguely familiar about him. His hair color and the way he stands. She feels as if she has seen him before but she can't place where. Maybe it is too many emotions' mixing with too much dancing that is causing her to lack the sense to be able to put two and two together. Whatever it is, something deep down tells her that it is important she figures out who this man is.

She nudges Jarreth in the arm. "Who is that?" she asks nodding her head in the direction of the man.

Jarreth looks bewildered and shrugs.

"He doesn't look like good news if you ask me," Drake says darkly from behind them.

Calandra turns to him and she senses that Drake somehow knows more than he is letting on, judging by the smirk on his face. Before she can push him for any answers, he winks, and turns and walks away into the night.

Chapter 20
True Colors

"You do know that I don't believe you for a second, right?" she asks Drake as they walk through the town together.

Jarreth wasn't particularly happy with the way she planned to try and get information out of Drake about the man in the pointed mask at the ball. But Calandra can't seem to shake the felling that it is extremely vital they find out exactly who it was. Jarreth insisted that he at least accompany her to put her plan into action, but she knew that Drake would be much less accommodating with him around. Surprisingly, Jarreth hadn't fought her on it, not as much as she had expected at least. Tristan had yet to show back up and Calandra had been fighting with her conscience, which was trying to remind her how much he meant to her and the huge apology that she owed him for the way she's been treating him.

"Have you developed a lie detecting power as well?" Drake sneers.

"Perhaps I have," she smiles at him and then remembers that she is a horrible liar.

"Oh my dear Calandra, you can't be more cunning than me, so don't even try!"

She feels slightly discouraged and wonders if her plan is actually going to get her anywhere. She had felt pretty confident when she left and headed over to Drake's house. But somehow, when she's not around Drake, she seems to forget just how good he is at deceiving and playing mind games. She has only just begun to learn to keep up in the Fae mind game department, and she is nowhere near the same level as Drake, or even Jarreth for that matter. She has a long ways to go in every aspect of this world. But something tells her that the mind game play is one talent she will never be able to learn to the same extent as Drake.

"Take me to the field," she tells him, deciding not to go along with his previous comment.

"For?"

"I want to learn more about my powers." She looks in front of her trying to be sure that her eyes won't give away her true intentions. "Jarreth still won't show me much of anything."

"Figured as much," Drake mumbles and turns their direction towards the field. "Luckily I had a good bit of fun the last time we were there alone," he winks at her. "So I'm more than happy to return with you anytime you'd like."

Calandra has to remember to keep her eye roll to herself and go along with the plan. She forces a smile and decides to kick things up a notch by taking his arm in hers as they walk. The field is back to normal without a single sign of the ball from a few nights ago. In a way, Calandra feels slightly disappointed to see it back in its original state. The lights had given it an extra boost of magic that had made it stunning. Although, she gets the feeling that the field would prefer to be in its current state than messed with in any way. Nature has a tendency to be vain, as Jarreth had explained to her after the ball.

Without even thinking about it or realizing what she was doing, Calandra walks straight over to the large tree in the field. Something about this tree always draws her in. She feels connected to it. It's a sort of magnetic pull that she can't, and doesn't want to fight. She puts her hand on the tree and lets its magic course through her. Her eyes close instinctively. Drake's hand is on her shoulder before she even realizes he is behind her.

"What is it?" She asks, once again feeling unable to form a coherent question. Luckily for her, it seems to be a faerie trait to read between the lines.

"Your draw to the tree?" Drake asks, leaning in much closer to her than he needs to.

Calandra nods. "It's just a tree, how can I feel it?"

"Just a tree?" Drake sounds surprised. "Calandra, it's not just a tree. It has a spirit. All plants do, they are living, breathing beings."

Calandra turns around and gauges his expression to judge if he is being serious or not. Sure enough, there is no sign of sarcasm, which is certainly a rarity for Drake. "So why me?"

"Who says it's just you?" Drake responds immediately, but a look flashes across his face and she wonders what it means.

"Is it?"

Drake shrugs, leaving Calandra wondering what he's not telling her. "I guess you'd need another human around to ask that question wouldn't you?" His sarcasm returns full force.

"So all of the humans left right after the ball?" She asks.

"Rules are rules," Drake replies nonchalantly.

"What is it that you need them for exactly?" Calandra realizes as soon as she asks the question that she's liable to regret it.

"Different things for different Fae, Calandra." Drake leaves the question unanswered and turns and walks a few feet away from her.

"Like?" Calandra presses further.

"Emotions."

"I know that one already, what are some of the others?"

"Looks for some, morality for others, vanity, blood–" he barely speaks the last word audibly.

"Blood?"

Drake nods.

"Like a vampire?"

"Not in the least!" Drake responds, he is clearly offended at the comparison. "Vampires need blood for food, it's their survival. Fae need it for— different reasons. We don't partake of it in the same way, it's more of a ritual for us."

"So vampires are real?"

"That's your question?" Drake arches an eyebrow at her.

Calandra shrugs feeling embarrassed and then giggles.

"You surprise me Calandra."

"Is that possible?"

"Of course it is, I can be— intrigued. My interest can be piqued. I'm not completely emotionless."

"Is there a reason for the tree and me?" She changes back to the original line of questioning, sensing that he is avoiding the latest question for some reason.

"Yes," he says simply.

"What is it?"

"That's not for you to know just yet I don't think."

"You know I'll just have Jarreth tell me," she scoffs.

"How do you know that he knows? You seem to have some mistaken idea that Jarreth and I know the same things when it comes to you. I have to wonder what exactly gave you that impression."

Calandra shrugs.

"You'd do well to remember that's not the case, not even close. Remember Jarreth was not the only one that was in the picture with Hollyn, so if you really want some answers you just might have to come to me, whether you like it or not."

Drake walks over to the center of the field where a group of Sprites dance around a left over rainbow tulip from the ball.

"Wanna play?" his voice changes completely, it turns boyish and mischievous.

Calandra is disturbed that her first instinct is to get excited and say yes. The desire doesn't go away, it sits in her chest, burning through her with the intensity of a forest fire. Suddenly, a new thought distracts her from it, at least momentarily. "What makes you think it's ok to mess with creatures like that?" she asks.

Drake shrugs, "why not?"

Calandra scoffs, "do you have any regard for feelings other than your own?"

"Faerie!" Drake replies simply. "Besides, for your information, I was asking in regards to your feelings. Don't pretend like you didn't enjoy our time here a few weeks ago." He smiles up at her mischievously as he says it.

The burning desire comes back full force. Calandra can't fight the smile from breaking through and she blushes along with it.

Drake's eyes seem to light up in response. "You don't have to hide it from me Calandra, I won't judge."

Calandra sits on the grass across from him. "Somehow, I feel you'd be the first to judge me."

Drake looks surprised and nods his head. "Calandra, evil doesn't judge, it only tempts, remember?" He taps her nose gently before turning his attention back to the Sprites playing between them. "Now, I asked you a question. Fun or no fun?"

A million different answers run through Calandra's mind, most of them the types of responses she should say, the ones that end in no. However, when her mouth opens, it betrays her and says the one that ends in yes. She instantly wants to take it back and say no, but it's no use. Her brain, heart, and mind aren't working in the same direction.

Drake's smile goes up a few notches in wickedness as he looks over at her. "I want you to try something," he says and he reaches his hand out to her.

Calandra looks at him skeptical of what to do. Memories of the last experience here flash through her and it sends a mixture of temptation and guilt pulsing through her. After a few moments, she realizes that fighting the urge is pointless. She sighs before she gives in and reaches out to take his hand.

He turns her hand over in his and faces her palm towards the ground. Holding her gaze, he lightly rubs his finger in small circles on her palm. A tickling sensation runs through her and mixes with the chill that his touch makes her feel. Just like that, he empties out her conscience. Drake holds her hand in midair for what seems like an eternity before he finally places it on the grass below them. "Close your eyes," he tells her.

Deep down in the pit of her stomach, Calandra knows she should be questioning what Drake is doing. Or more likely, she should be running the other way. But she ignores that instinct. Instead she has an inclination to discover what he will show her. Her anticipation rises and she obliges his request and closes her eyes.

"Listen to your surroundings," he whispers into her ear, he is somehow suddenly behind her.

Her breath catches somewhere between her stomach and her throat and she has to steady herself again. After refocusing, she is able to concentrate on what she was asked to do. The feel of the grass against her skin sends tickles through her as she allows nature to fill her and course through her.

"Remember how to focus that to do what you want it to?"

Calandra nods, "what am I doing with it?"

"Just let it go," he says softly into her ear. "I don't want you to try and direct it to anything in particular. Just let it go and see what happens."

Calandra doesn't understand where he is going with this, but she does as he says anyways. She focuses on all of the feelings inside her and all at once lets them go through her hand, she lifts her hand up off the ground and feels it release through her fingers.

She opens her eyes to find flowers covering the field, there are so many that not a single blade of grass shows anymore. The ones closest to her are multicolored, like the ones that were scattered during the ball. She turns around and notices that the flowers surrounding where Drake sits behind her are all black roses. A shudder runs through her when she notices the difference. Further out from where they sit, the flowers turn into a beautiful mixture of blue, purple, and pink lilies. The scene takes Calandra's breath away until she realizes that the sprites are frozen in front of her. Her heart sinks. She thought she had done something beautiful this time in making the flowers, and somehow unknowingly, she also did something ugly.

"Relax Calandra," Drake says as he comes

back around her to sit in front of her again, bringing them face to face. "I did the sprites, you did the rest."

Something lifts inside her with the relief that she wasn't the one that caused their stand still. But it unsettles when it hits her that there is no need for them to be frozen. Drake simply did it for spite, for some sick pleasure. She lifts her hand towards the sprites and musters up the little bit of strength she needs to unfreeze them.

Drake looks disappointed. "It doesn't hurt them, you know?" he says simply.

"That's not the point Drake, you don't have the right to toy with creatures like that."

Drake rolls his eyes and gets up. He looks down at her once more, his expression is unreadable and he turns and walks away without another word. Calandra sighs in his absence. So much for her plan, she hadn't managed to get any useful information out of him, Jarreth had been right...again.

One of the sprites lands on her shoulder, she must be forgiven from the last time she was here when she had been the one to toy with them. "Sorry," she mumbles under her breath and lies down in the grass. A shadow appears over her and startles her upright again. Tristan stands behind her and looks timidly down at her.

"Hey," he says under his breath.

"Hi, you spying on me?" She asks irritated as she lies back down on the ground.

Tristan sighs and sits on the ground next to her, reminiscent of their time in the field in the mortal world and how far away they seem to be from those people now.

"Not spying," he says, "just checking up on you."

"I don't need to be checked up on Tristan."

"You sure about that?"

Calandra sits up and glares at him, "yes," She says flatly.

"Hmm."

"What? What could you possibly be getting at here?"

"Just seems like you may need someone to be checking up on you and your interactions with

Drake."

Calandra opens her mouth to respond, but nothing comes out. She sighs and lies back down.

They sit in silence for several long moments. Calandra's eyes are closed and she refuses to give into Tristan.

"You know he's dangerous right?" Tristan finally cuts into the silence.

"Of course I do Tristan." Calandra keeps her eyes closed and rolls them to herself.

"So why do you still let him influence you that way?"

Calandra remains silent while she tries to find a way to respond to that. "I don't know," she finally says with a sigh.

Truthfully, she doesn't know. She knows that she shouldn't do anything Drake tells her to, yet somehow something deep within her draws her listen to him anyways. Maybe Drake was right earlier, maybe it is purely temptation. Temptation and darkness embodied, that is what Drake is after all. Then again, Jarreth could have been overreacting when he told her that.

"You know bad company corrupts good character, right Cal?"

"No Tristan, I don't know and you certainly don't know. Just stop with the guilt trip again, I'm not in the mood right now!" She didn't mean to snap, but snap is what she did. She can't imagine going through another talk like what they had at the ball.

Tristan stares at her in disbelief. "I guess this isn't exactly easy for you, I mean you wouldn't want your new friends to think badly of you or anything," he says firmly.

"I'm sorry," she says, "I didn't mean to—"

"I know Calandra," he scoots into her and holds his arm out.

Calandra smiles and leans into him. She takes in his comfort as she has so many times before. She lets him hold her and tries to pretend for the moment that things are ok, normal even. Tristan traces circles along her back. "Calandra?"

"Please don't." She looks down at the ground, unable to bring herself to look at him.

He looks down at her with sadness in his

eyes. It's a disappointment that breaks her just a little bit more. "Are you really ok?" Tristan asks her, sincerity written all over his face.

Calandra pulls herself away from him and is suddenly aware that she is using him in a way she shouldn't be. She realizes that this interaction means more to Tristan than it does to her. He's getting the idea that she's changing back to who she used to be and she knows she's not. As if she hasn't already put him through enough already.

"I will be," she shrugs.

"You are strong," he informs her.

"No Tristan, not really. I always fall apart and you put the pieces back together for me, remember?"

"Maybe it's time you learn how to put yourself back together Cal? You've always known how to, you only think you need someone to fix it for you."

Calandra smiles, somehow reassured. "I'm sorry I couldn't get him to let you go, I really did try." She changes the subject, afraid to go down that road with him.

"I guess I'm starting to get used to this place," he shrugs.

"It's not exactly terrible," she smiles.

"Not at all." Tristan's eyes fill with a longing, a sense that he's getting through to her finally.

"So, I guess I'll see you around." She gets up and dusts herself off.

"You're leaving?" He looks up at her, confused.

She nods. "It's time to get back," she says simply. "Are you staying here?"

Tristan shrugs and doesn't move to get up.

"Bye Tristan." She says and without another word walks away and heads back to the clubhouse, hoping that Jarreth isn't there at the moment, she would like some time alone tonight to just think.

Chapter 21
Vision

A familiar dense, gray fog rolls in. Everything clouds over and grows colder in its presence. The air feels thick around her and she can't make anything out other than a few shadows. Her head feels like it's being pressurized from the inside out. Her eyes close automatically against the feeling and it instantly clears out. She opens her eyes slowly to find that the fog is gone and simply a dense mist remains.

The field lies in front of her. It's early morning, the sun is still rising in the distance. The sky is tinged a euphoric mixture of pinks, oranges, and yellows. There are beads of dew on each blade of grass and the sunlight reflects against it to create a beautiful scene. Calandra could stand here and stare at it all day, until a shadow catches the corner of her eye.

She looks in the direction of it and is shocked to see a man that seems oddly familiar standing in the field and he seems to be staring straight at her. Her body forgets how to breathe, or move, or think clearly, it simply freezes. They stare at each other for what seems like an eternity. A voice from behind her makes Calandra realize that it's not her the man is staring at after all.

"Long time no see." The voice behind her is familiar, she knows she's heard it before. But at the moment, her body is still unwilling to react from the shock of seeing this stranger here, much less turn to see who the voice belongs to.

"I'm back for good!" The stranger replies to the person behind Calandra.

"We'll see," the voice counters.

"Oh ye of little faith." The stranger seems more than a little surprised by the attitude coming from the voice.

"You know that she is here now, or you wouldn't have come back."

"I do."

"And you still think you have a chance? She was marked, as soon as she crossed over."

Calandra suddenly processes that they are discussing her. The realization also pushes through for her who the voice coming from behind her is.

"No matter," the stranger shrugs.

"We'll see," Drake replies again.

Her body finally wakes up from the shock that it's been in and she is able to turn and verify that it is in fact Drake standing behind her. He is dressed in his all black attire as usual, and his eyes look darker than normal, much more purple than lavender.

"She was born to stop you Kailen, and you know that, so why do you insist on trying still?" Drake's smile is sly and he has a smug confidence about him.

"Prophecies aren't always true you know?" Kailen responds.

"More often than not," Drake counters.

"Maybe, but in case you haven't noticed, this is a special situation, so I just may have a chance after all. Have you managed to get her on your side yet?"

Calandra turns to look at Drake whose face has gone sheet white. His eyes are holding steady at their normal lavender color and Calandra waits for him to answer. Everything suddenly dissolves around her and she is surrounded by the tree house. Of course as soon as she finally starts to process things, the vision ends. Go figure.

"Cal?" Jarreth is sitting next to her, his eyes are concerned as he leans in and inspects her.

"I'm fine," she assures him, "I could use some tea though." She doesn't even mean to say the last part, it comes out on it's own accord.

Jarreth instantly jumps up and heads into the kitchen.

"And after I get some, you'll explain the vision?" He asks sounding unsure.

Calandra nods and Jarreth continues into the kitchen.

****

Calandra's surroundings have changed once more. Only this time it was of her own accord, she now sits in Drake's living room. She can't keep the memories of her last visit here out of her head. Jarreth had insisted they come and discuss her vision with Drake after she explained what she had seen to him. Tristan had tried to leave when her and Jarreth arrived, but she begged him to stay. She knows deep down that it was wrong to do so, but some part of her needs him here for support.

Drake sits on the left side of Calandra, his legs are crossed over each other and he is leaned into the couch, he looks utterly relaxed. Jarreth is on her right side, his entire body is tensed, as per his usual when he is around Drake. Tristan is off to the other side of the room in the small wooden chair, his expression is unreadable and his body is cloaked in shadows.

"So you finally figured it out?" Drake chuckles.

"Who is he and when is he coming?" Calandra asks.

"Why do you assume that the vision is the future?" Drake smiles coyly.

Calandra looks over to Jarreth, confused. She didn't know she could have visions of the past, the only other one she had experienced was of the future. She once again made assumptions, which she was quickly learning she shouldn't be making in this world as nothing seems to add up the way you think it will. How far in the past could it have been? For a quick moment, she wonders if it had taken place before she had even arrived. Then she remembers Drake's line about her mark and is slightly relieved in knowing that it couldn't have been that far back.

"When?" Jarreth finally breaks the silence.

"The ball."

"He was at the ball?" Calandra squeals.

Drake nods, "I told you the mystery man didn't look like good news didn't I?"

"Who is he and how was I born to stop him?" Calandra can't quite figure out why she's as shocked as she is, this is Drake after all. *Sin and temptation*, she reminds herself. "Stop him from what exactly?" Nothing makes sense and no one seems to be willing to cooperate and give her any help.

"I didn't see what difference it would make for you to know his name since you still wouldn't have had a clue who he was," Drake shrugs to belittle it even further.

"What is he doing? What prophesy?" The questions come out little by little without making any sense.

"Calandra," Tristan's voice seems to have a warning behind it, which finally sends Calandra over the edge completely.

"Don't start with me!" She snaps at him.

"Why am I even here in the first place? You

made me stay for what exactly?"

"I don't know!" The truth slips out harsher than she intended it. She knows if it weren't for the shadows she would see the hurt all over his face. She's just cut him deep, she can feel it in the room. Without another word, Tristan gets up and leaves the house. Something tells Calandra to go after him, but she fights the urge. What can she say at this point? She's done nothing but stomp all over him and use him since this whole ordeal started. Unfortunately for Tristan, the trend doesn't seem like it's going to let up anytime soon either.

In her distraction of Tristan's breakdown, Calandra didn't see Drake leave the room, but he returns with a cup of tea. Her first impulse is to say thanks, until she remembers that he is what caused the stress that made her need the drink in the first place. She gives a quick, timid smile instead.

"What does he want?" Jarreth asks.

"Like you don't know." Drake replies instantly.

"Um, I don't!" Calandra chimes in looking back and forth between the two of them.

Drake nods his head towards Jarreth signaling for him to be the one to explain.

Calandra starts in on her drink to prepare for what may be coming.

"He's here to prevent you from stopping him," Jarreth says simply.

"Yeah, thanks for clearing that up Jare!" Calandra rolls her eyes at him as she begins in on her tea.

"Kailen was the reason behind the downfall of Faerie, he was the human that Echo fell in love with that caused all of this to happen. Only he's not exactly human anymore."

"What does that even mean?"

"No one's totally sure." Drake jumps in. "He was human when he was here, when he fell in love with Echo. Then after the veil got closed and he was taken away from Echo, he went a little—crazy?"

"He's completely ruthless Calandra, he has no heart, and more than likely no soul. I wouldn't be surprised if he made a deal with the devil himself to be able to come back for revenge." Jarreth takes the explanation down a slightly different path and causes it to make even less sense.

"Exactly how heartless is this man?" She asks before she downs the rest of her drink. "Like Drake heartless?"

"I would be hurt," Drake insists, "if I had a heart that is." He smiles mechanically.

"Worse," Jarreth says.

Calandra holds her empty cup out to Drake insisting he go refill it for her again. He rolls his eyes, but takes the cup and leaves the room anyway.

Jarreth puts his arm on her shoulder. "You ok?"

Calandra shrugs.

Drake returns and hands Calandra her cup.

"So are you guys figuring out a plan or forming some sort of spiritual connection over here?" he asks.

Calandra rolls her eyes, "still butt hurt over

the heartless comment are we?"

Jarreth clears his throat and they both stop talking. "Do you know exactly what Kailen plans to do?" He asks Drake.

Drake shrugs, "not exactly, we're not on the best of terms at the moment."

"Oh really?" Jarreth seems unbelieving of this. "And why is that?"

Calandra almost chokes on her drink when she remembers the vision. "Because he didn't take his side, he told him I was going to win," she smiles.

Jarreth looks at her confused, "he also was working with Kailen and trying to get you on his side, remember?"

Drake rolls his eyes. "Don't let your head get all big sweetie, it had nothing to do with you."

"So what do we do?" Jarreth changes the subject quickly.

"Trust me," Drake starts, "when Kailen is ready for you to act, you'll know. He obviously doesn't have a plan yet or he would've already acted on it."

"So we do nothing?" Calandra asks.

"Precisely," Drake replies, "don't draw attention to yourself before it's necessary. Figure it out when the time comes."

Calandra gulps down the rest of her drink.

"You won't be alone when he does decide to show up Calandra, we'll do this together, I promise." Jarreth smiles reassuringly and Drake scoffs in the background.

Calandra knows it's a promise that he can't really make, but she allows herself to take solace in it regardless.

Chapter 22
Return

You won't have to face him alone. Calandra knew it was a promise he couldn't truly make, but it doesn't make her feel any better now that she stares at Kailen face to face. Jarreth had gone to town to pick up some things for the house since no one seemed to want Calandra to leave her house for reasons that hadn't been fully disclosed to her, as usual.

Kailen's eyes are dark midnight blue and opaque. His hair is copper and his skin is much paler than should be possible. He is dressed in all gray. They stand across from each other outside, just in front of the tree house. Calandra backed herself into the door when she saw him standing there after she stepped out to explore the land a bit. Her heart races faster than she knew was possible.

"I take it they filled you in on exactly who I am," Kailen says coolly.

No one has filled her in on anything exactly since she's been here. It's all been a frustrating series of riddles and pieces that they've chosen to disclose. "For the most part." Calandra decides to play it cool and pretend to know more than she actually does.

"And you know who you are then?"

"I'm Calandra." So much for playing it cool, she had managed to say the dumbest thing possible. She knew that wasn't what he meant by his statement, but her mind didn't have time to stop her mouth from saying the words regardless.

"Yeah— I feel like there's still some things you're unaware of," Kailen smiles coyly.

Calandra stares at him blankly, trying to decide what to say and hoping she doesn't manage to make herself seem even more clueless than she already had. "Why should I trust you to tell me?"

"We both want the same thing Calandra."

"What's that?" She vows to give Jarreth and Drake a nice chewing if she gets through this little show down. If they had explained everything to her, she wouldn't have to make herself out to be a total dimwit right now.

"This," Kailen motions his arms around him as he says it, "Faerie."

Someone must have forgotten to tell him that Calandra hadn't asked for any of this. Before she has a chance to even try to think of something to say, Kailen starts in again.

"You see, I couldn't allow the same creatures that destroyed me and took away everything that I'd ever had that was good away from me, keep this beautiful world all to themselves, that wouldn't be justice now would it? I vowed to come back somehow and give them all exactly what they deserved. If you only knew everything I had to go to in order to make this happen." His eyes gleam an odd color at her and it sets her nerves on fire.

"What are you exactly?"

"You'll find out when everyone else does, I suppose. What I am will be plenty powerful enough to put every one of these horrid creatures out of their little fantasy world of being able to treat humans like they're nothing and they don't matter. What I am is enough to take the power away from them, and watch them starve without human interaction, watch them suffer as their life source drowns out of them slowly."

"So, you want to replace evil with evil? That seems like the perfect plan." Suddenly Calandra is completely sick of the games and she feels a new confidence wash over her. "What exactly are you here to discuss Kailen?"

Calandra tries to let everything soak in, she

tries to make some sense of it all. Something still doesn't seem to add up all the way. She still can't put her finger on why she's so powerful. Why she has been so quick to adapt to the world. Why is she the one who will be able to fix everything? She still has no clue what the prophecy is, or how it is that she seems to have inherited much more Fae than human. There is still a piece to this puzzle that is missing. There is something no one is telling her. Maybe something that no one knows, but either way she knows she needs to figure this out before she can put an end to anything.

"Well, seeing as we're both after the same thing. I thought that some lines should be drawn, so to speak," he turns back to face her and stops walking around.

"No lines." Calandra finally decides to pull strength from her powers and toughen up despite the confusion coursing through her mind.

"No? So what do you propose then? You know I'm not going to just stand by and watch you try and take over as if you deserve it."

"You can't correct a wrong with another

wrong." Did she just repeat one of her father's corny parenting sayings? She must be going over the deep end completely. "Seeing as I have destiny on my side, I think I'll be just fine either way." She gives a snide smile after to add a nice sarcastic note to it.

"Destiny?" Kailen scoffs, "is that what they told you?"

"No, that's what this told me." She pulls her pink baby-doll tee off of her shoulder and exposes her dragonfly.

"Sorry to tell you deary, but that means nothing." His words are instant but he can't hide the stunned expression on his face.

Calandra rolls her eyes at his new way to refer to her. She knows that he's just trying to get under her skin, unfortunately despite that knowledge, it's working. Her temper is rising under her skin, she feels it starting towards its boiling point, and she feels very close to breaking down completely.

"Did you call them?" Kailen once again brings her back to the present moment and

Calandra realizes they are surrounded by Sprites. He looks impressed, at least to a small extent.

Calandra isn't sure if she had called them, she certainly hadn't meant to if so. But to admit that would show yet another weakness and she has already managed to expose too many of those in this encounter. She nods in agreement instead.

"And what do you suppose they are going to do for you exactly?"

The Sprites gather around her staying behind her just slightly. The soft buzzing of their wings is much more comforting than she could have ever expected it to be. Instead of answering his question, she is suddenly inspired to try another route. Since talking seems to be her weakness and give away too many of her faults, she decides to try a more intimidating way about things. She's simply going to stare and look resolved with her Sprite supporters behind her.

"Oh, how nice of you to join us," Kailen rolls his eyes as he says it.

Calandra turns around and is more than

comforted to see Jarreth has returned. He takes a place next to Calandra and her confidence increases tenfold. "Kailen." Jarreth says the name with even more hate than he uses when he says Drake's name. This surprises Calandra.

"Jarreth." Kailen returns the hatred.

There is a beyond awkward and uncomfortable stare off. Too many thoughts run through Calandra's head and she feels her emotions threaten to come off balance again. She knows she can't risk loosing it again. She feels much more in control with Jarreth by her side, but she's still too much on edge to think that he's enough to keep her in check completely.

"Kailen," Calandra finds her voice and starts in, "what exactly did you come over here to tell me? Enough with the games, get it out so that you can get out."

"Well," Kailen smiles approvingly, "I thought you might want to know that I decided to play a little game."

Of course he did. Faeries love games. It is something Calandra is still learning, and at the current moment, something she isn't liking in the least.

"What kind of game?" She gives in, not knowing what other choice she really has in the matter.

"A game of hide and seek. I hid something that you want and now you have to seek it." His smile is beyond wicked, it borders on the line of insane.

Calandra's first instinct is to ask what he hid, but she knows she doesn't need to ask. She already knows. Her very first vision comes into mind. Tristan. Because she hadn't put him through enough already. Because he wasn't upset with her enough. Because she didn't suddenly need him now more than ever. Kailen must somehow know all of this. Jarreth automatically reaches out and takes her hand. The electric current pulses through her and gives her the strength she so desperately needs.

"Rules?" She asks simply.

"There are none," Kailen says. Calandra doesn't buy it for a second.

"I'm not ready to make my move just yet Calandra. This is simply a little fun for me and to make sure you know exactly what I am capable of."

"And for you to see that I can take you!" She manages to put much more confidence into her voice than she actually feels at the moment.

"If you say so." Kailen starts to walk away but turns back around. "Enjoy!" He smiles again, "I look forward to much more encounters dearest." He stands there looking menacing but doesn't budge at all.

"You may go," Jarreth says tightly.

Kailen's smile widens, "and what if I'm not ready?"

Calandra is beyond sick of the twisted games here. Too many emotions are coursing through her as it is and now he wants to play some more. "Go!" She laces her voice with as much evil as she can muster up.

Kailen laughs.

Pulling from everything that boils within her at the moment, Calandra reaches into the deepest parts of her. She feels it building and yielding to whatever she wills for it to do. All at once she lifts her arm towards Kailen and holds her palm out towards him. Crimson sparks shoot out of her and Kailen is lifted into the air and thrown at least 20 feet back. He is taken aback completely. The Sprites leave their post by Calandra and head off towards Kailen. He leaves in a hurry with the Sprites seeing him off.

Jarreth looks proud. It's a look she hasn't seen on him yet and it very much suits him. "That was amazing," he says, "how did you do it?"

Calandra shrugs as if it's no big deal. It doesn't seem like that big of a deal at the moment. It doesn't change anything. Her world is still currently beyond messed up and now she has to worry about finding Tristan.

"You already know where he is," Jarreth says, sensing where her thoughts are taking her.

"Not really," she says sadly.

"Calandra, you saw it in a vision. You can find the place I promise you. After what I just saw, you can apparently do much more than anyone knows or ever would've expected."

This suddenly makes her feel better. She allows herself this small victory. Takes in the accomplishment that she has just made and feels proud of herself. The rest she can figure out in a minute, for now she wants to feel empowered.

Chapter 23
Save You

Jarreth had been right, again. Calandra had a feeling that could get old fast. Once she focused on the vision and concentrated on the surroundings in it she had been able to lead them to the location easily. However, now that they stand outside of the cave and she knows what she will see once they walk inside, the accomplishment she felt from being able to lead them here suddenly dwindles down.

"Are you ready for this?" Jarreth asks softly.

"I don't think I'll ever be ready for this," she shrugs.

"You're not alone, remember that," he smiles.

"Not at all." Another voice comes from behind them, one that wasn't supposed to be here.

"Drake," Calandra rolls her eyes. She doesn't have to turn around to see who was behind them, she knows that voice.

"Did you really think I would miss the show down?"

"Sorry to tell you but you already missed it." She informs him with more pleasure than it should have brought her.

"I don't care about the one with you and Kailen," he says, "this one on the other hand, well, I think it should be rather interesting."

Calandra looks to Jarreth hoping for more information, but his expression is blank as well.

Great. Here she thought that having the vision had prepared her for what was to come, she hasn't prepared for any surprises. She doesn't want any surprises, not that she wanted any of this in the first place.

She turns back to the cave and tries to prepare herself to go inside. She has faced some sort of evil incarnate already today. A few days ago she would have thought that would been impossible for her, but she had done it and even over powered him in the end. Yet despite knowing she had overcome that, facing Tristan tied up in a dark, damp cave still seems beyond impossible. She remembers how cold Tristan was in the vision, she hadn't been able to figure out at the time why he was acting that way. Different, that was the word he had chosen to describe her. Now she knows exactly what he meant by it. And she knows what Drake wants to see. There is going to be a show down. Tristan is finally going to give her exactly what she deserves. Her heart deflates in her chest.

"I think I should go in alone," she turns to

face Jarreth and Drake.

Jarreth nods as if he had expected her to do that all along. Drake looks disappointed but he doesn't appear to want to challenge her. She takes a deep breath and pulls from within before she turns and enters the cave still feeling completely unprepared for what lies ahead.

The cave is just as beautiful as it was in the vision. It seems wrong to be in a place this amazingly designed and be expecting something so horrible to take place in its beauty. Tristan is against the back wall, his face is dirty, his eyes are tired, and tear tracks streak through the dirt on his face. His hands are behind his back as if he is tied up. His legs are stretched out in front of him.

"Calandra," his voice is hoarse, "wouldn't you be a sight for sore eyes if you weren't so—different."

It's her vision all over again. What scares her now is what may happen afterwards, her vision was so short it didn't give her much insight into what to expect. Water drips off of parts of the cave and sends echoes throughout the cave.

"Are you ok?" She asks as she walks over to him.

She kneels down in front of him and reaches for his arms. She can't see anything tying them up, but he is bound by something. She pulls at his arms and feels the resistance against whatever spell is holding him there.

"I'm just peachy," he says coldly.

She pulls a few more times before realizing what she needs to do to get him out. She steadies her thoughts and emotions and focuses on willing her powers. Crimson shoots out of her fingers and his arms are immediately released. He pulls them in front of him and rubs his wrists. Calandra sits on the damp ground and leans into the wall behind them. She feels the moisture soak into her clothes and onto her skin. It chills her to the bone, but she resists the urge to get back up. She sighs, closes her eyes, and leans her head against the wall pushing away the thoughts of what it will do to her hair.

How can she tell him what she had become

without scarring him? She knows what she feels, and there is no way to get around burning him. After everything he had done and everything she'd already put him through, none of it is fair to him. Calandra can feel her words forming the knife that will slice his heart to pieces. That alone is enough to break her own heart. Tristan closes his eyes, he can feel something is wrong, he knows her too well.

There is no way to put it off, no way to lie. She just has to come right out and say it. She opens her mouth to begin slicing his heart open, but he puts his hand up before the words came out.

"Don't say it. I already know where this is going, and I don't want to hear it." He looks at the ground as he speaks.

She is glad he isn't looking at her, the pain that she knows is in his eyes would only make this ordeal that much more impossible. "What do you mean you know?" She finally manages to ask.

"I felt something was wrong. I sensed the change, a drift in the winds, and I felt you get carried away along with it. Away from me and away from Him, the one that you really need to save you." His voice cracks as he adds the last part.

She knows what is coming next. She knows the tears are coming for him. She had known for much longer than she is willing to admit that this was going to happen. She just wasn't sure until this moment exactly how it would happen and now she is going to lose Tristan completely. She is scared he'll never even want to look at her again. No matter what she feels about anything, she knows she will always need Tristan in her life and by her side. Despite those feelings and despite everything they have been through together, she doesn't feel sad. She isn't upset, she is just here doing what she knows she has to do.

Tristan finally looks up at her, and she's surprised to see that there are no tears in his eyes, it is anger. "I can't be the one to save you Calandra, there's only one Savior, and it certainly isn't me. It's like a drug to you isn't it? The power, the games, the mind control. You've beat me down over and over and when it gets the best of you, you just know I'll still be standing here waiting to drag you out of that hole. I won't watch you go through this cycle again, I won't save you this time. I can't. I'm done being your fix when I'm the one who gets hurt in the end Calandra."

The words cut through her chest and she feels her heart shatter into pieces and land in the pit of her stomach. He is right, and that realization brings on the sting of tears that tries to break through the mask of nonchalantness she has been wearing for so long. She fights them down. She starts to open her mouth to rebuke him, but nothing comes out. Nothing she can say will matter after that, but she owes him something. In this moment, Calandra realizes just how selfish she has been. She has broken Tristan's heart, and yet some part of her still wants him to keep fighting for her despite it being a loosing battle.

Calandra sighs and looks to the ground. "You're right," she looks back at him.

His eyes cut deep into her soul, there's an anxiousness in them. He's waiting for her to tell him she will change, that she will be the person she was before. The hope sits plainly in his expression and his desperation is apparent.

"I really am so sorry. I don't want to lose you Tristan, you're my best friend and I need you." She pleads to him, her voice filled with sincerity. "I didn't mean for any of this to happen. I promise you I never meant to hurt you." She feels the tears coming to the surface, and she fights with everything she has to keep them at bay. "I just— everything's so different here. I'm different here. This place is changing me, and even though I wasn't looking to change, it feels good. There's nothing I can do to stop it, and quite honestly, I don't want to."

The disappointment makes itself clear on his face as he stares back at her. He opens his mouth as if he is going to say something, but he closes it back immediately. "The world you're in shouldn't matter Calandra. I don't care if you woke up as Alice in the looking glass, what you believe and what you know is right shouldn't change regardless."

Calandra stands up and dusts herself off. She makes an effort to not look at Tristan, afraid she might finally break down if she does. "So I guess you're going back home now?" Calandra decides to change the subject.

"I think I'll try staying for a little bit," he shrugs and watches her as she paces in front of him. She finally stops with her body angled towards the exit of the cave. "Someone's gotta look after you since you've forgotten how to look after yourself."

Calandra smiles softly and turns away from Tristan and begins the walk out of the cave. Her body draws back to look back at him but she won't allow it. She can't bear to see the disappointment on his face. Not that her heart can break anymore, but her soul still can and she can't allow that to happen. With every bit of strength she has left in her, she forces herself to walk away.

"Then I guess I'll see you around. If you

want that is, or not if you don't," she whispers as she walks out of the cave and leaves him behind.

Tristan is gone, not completely gone, but in the sense that she's always known him in. The realization of it sends a tinge of pain through her. It's not quite as much pain as she knows she should feel given the circumstances, but it is there. She wonders where she's supposed to go from here, what she's supposed to do. She has just walked away from her safeguard. As this information washes over her, she sees Jarreth standing in the sunlight. Drake is gone, which makes her feel a bit more at ease.

"Did you scare him off?" She asks, suddenly feeling much lighter than she was just a few moments ago. Something about having finally told Tristan and having the confrontation out of the way is like a huge weight lifted off of her shoulders.

"Once you denied him the show, he left on his own."

"Lovely," she scoffs as she closes the remaining distance between them.

"Everything ok?" he asks sincerely.

"It's— handled," she can't think of a better word to use to describe the situation.

Jarreth slowly leans into her, holding her gaze as he closes the short distance between them, her emotions and the stress of the situation slowly drain away from her with his gaze. "So, now what?" he asks. Jarreth pulls her into his side and begins to lead them back towards Calandra's tree house.

"Now, I guess we see what happens, and where this all takes us," she says knowing that she's oversimplifying the situation.

They walk out into the sunset. The pink and lavender lights shine around them as they walk arm in arm. Her life is nothing like it had been weeks ago. Yet, at the current moment she doesn't mind. She is excited about it and ready to see where it will go. She doesn't know what is going to happen from here. She has no clue what lies ahead of her, of them, of the world of Faerie. But it all feels like right, it is her destiny. So, with a newfound confidence, she walks with her destiny to embrace the new Calandra and discover exactly what she is meant to become and what the prophecy that somehow regards her birth and her purpose is.

LAINY LANE

Epilogue
Ghost of You

Have you ever felt like you were in a completely hopeless situation? Like you tried everything in your power, exhausted all of your means, to get where you wanted to be, but you were still left simply watching your hopes and dreams pass you by? This is what has become of Tristan's life. He is in an unfamiliar world where he knows no one. Well, he knows one person. The love of his life is here. Yet he is forced to watch as day after day she walks around in the casing of the person that he knows and loves. He watches her laugh and smile and carry on like everything is perfect and content in the world.

But everything is not okay. He had her, she was his. And through no fault of his own, he lost her. Of course most men say they didn't do anything to lose their women, and usually its just denial. But in this case, it is true. He really had done nothing, yet he has still lost everything that's ever meant anything to him. That's the problem though, he hasn't lost it completely, but sometimes he wishes he had.

He can't help but wonder if it would hurt less if she was just gone or if he actually left. But he's still in her life, just as her friend. She still comes to him with her problems. And he pretends that he's okay with the situation and helps her figure out her issues. Somehow she doesn't see that it kills him inside every time she does this and he would never dream of telling her.

He feels haunted. After all those months, he had the impression that he knew her, that he had her figured out. But here he sits, alone, as he watches a complete stranger walk around in his true love's body. He watches as she tramples over his heart daily. He watches the ghost of who she used to be, who they were, follow her around constantly. It is taunting of what once was, what should still be, but what isn't anymore. What he desires the most, yet what he can no longer have.

Haunted. That is Tristan's life now. These are the thoughts that keep him up at night. These are the things that he can't get out of his head. The reason he has no time alone. He can't even keep track of time anymore. He isn't entirely sure how long he's been here. As of now, it seems like an eternity.

He sits against a tree with pink firework leaves blooming from it. The blue flowers on the ground around him look like butterflies and he finds himself wondering if they would actually turn into butterflies and fly away if he were to sit still long enough. He has seen Jarreth and

Calandra sit here many times, he's watched as they enjoy their picnics and tease each other about nonsense. Even though he sits here alone now, he can still see the memories of them play out right in front of him as if they were here.

    He closes his eyes against the thoughts and the images that have haunted him since the cave and show no sign of letting up anytime soon. He needs a distraction. He knows nothing will heal him from losing Calandra, but if he can at least find something to take the edge off of the pain, things would at least be a bit more bearable. But he can't think of anything capable of distracting him from such a pain. He catches a glimpse of someone walking towards him. At first he ignores it, until the sweet scent of honeysuckle catches his nose and causes him to look back up.

    Long brown curls frame her exquisite face. She is tall and slender and wears a white dress that flows along her figure while it drifts with the wind that surrounds her. He doesn't feel a breeze where he sits, but there is wind that picks up her dress and makes it flap around her ankles as she seemingly glides towards him. Her smile as she approaches is intoxicating. It combines with the smell of honeysuckle, a reminder of innocent childhood days, and he is completely enthralled by the new being that draws near him.

He doesn't realize he's staring until she reaches him, but he finds himself unable to stop. Gawk is probably a better word for what he is doing. She looks down for a moment before she joins him in the grass. She holds one hand out towards him. Her long nails are painted a light pink shade that reminds him of Calandra's lips.

"Trinity," she says melodically and her smile widens.

He has to close his eyes against the thought of Calandra and pushes it away as he puts his hand in hers. She grips it tightly as they shake hands. Despite his eyes being closed, he can feel that her eyes are on him. He brings himself out of his thoughts and pulls his gaze up to meet hers.

"Tristan," he says quieter than he intended.

Their hands drop from each other's. She

sits across from him and she puts her hands behind her and leans back into them to support herself as she lets the soft pink light of the sunset light her semi-transparent skin.

"Nice day isn't it?" She asks as she closes her eyes and takes a deep breath of the air around her in.

Tristan shrugs.

"You know, your face is far too appealing to show such sorrow." She opens her eyes momentarily and glances over at him before she turns back to the sky and closes her eyes once more.

To his surprise, the comment makes an annoyance build up in him. Like he needs this girl trying to flatter him along with everything else he has going on in his head. It doesn't matter how pretty she is or how sweet she smells, he is simply not in the mood for compliments, or company for that matter. He is in the mood to sulk. But just as he decides to get up and find another place to melt into his sorrows, his attitude changes completely.

Trinity lifts her arms off the ground and sits up straight. She takes in a deep breath and the air twists around her, it picks up her curls and makes them float mid-air but they still frame her face. She hums a soft tune as she places one hand on the grass directly under her shoulders. The moment her hand touches the ground, everything changes.

Tristan suddenly doesn't care about his pain anymore, he only cares about her. She is intoxicatingly beautiful and her smell is completely enthralling. The thoughts in his head finally dissipate and the images that have haunted him for weeks now are gone. For the first time since the cave, a real smile comes across his face. This isn't one of the fake smiles that he has been putting on for Calandra. It is a real, sincere smile. He feels uplifted. His heart is light and free again. He is happy and pain free.

He doesn't know how she had made it happen and he immediately decides he doesn't really care, he can breathe freely in the absence of the pain. That realization sets off another, he knows that he can't allow it stop. He can't feel the pain again. He needs this, he deserves to feel happy again. He turns and looks at her in exasperation from the being freed of his haunting of emotions.

"Your welcome," she says before he has a chance to say anything.

"Who are you?" He asks.

"I told you already," she chuckles, "Trinity."

"That's not what I meant," he scoffs.

Trinity stands up and for a second Tristan swears he catches a glimpse of small light blue wings just above her shoulder blades. He shakes his head to clear the image from his head.

"Come with me and I will explain everything you want to know and more," she smiles in a way that turns her statement into a dare, "I know all about the prophecy, I can tell you everything that you need to get her back." She turns and in one swift movement starts to walk away. Her hand gestures behind her back inviting him to follow after her. He starts to get up and then stops himself momentarily to make himself wonder what he is doing exactly.

But now that he no longer sees the baby blue wings descending from her back, he can't think of a reason to stop himself. He is far too captivated to turn back now. She has taken the pain that has plagued him for weeks now and she has a way for him to get Calandra back and away from the devils she's been surrounding herself with. That's all that he hears and his excitement manages to block out all the other warnings surrounding Trinity. He stands and runs to close the distance she has already created. He doesn't know who she is, where she is taking him, what she is, or why exactly he is following her. All he knows is at the moment, he doesn't have a choice. He feels like he has to find out, and finding out means following her, wherever that may lead.

LAINY LANE

About The Author
Lainy Lane

Lainy Lane is a 27-year-old mother of 2 beautiful girls, one of which is now the family guardian angel. She has a wonderful husband that is a large part of the reason she is where she is today. She has always had an obsession with fantasy worlds. When she was younger, she always said that Peter Pan would be the perfect man because when things got rough, he could whisk you away to Neverland, where all your problems would simply disappear. As she grew up, she learned the harsh reality that life can be cruel, and no world (even fantasy ones) is completely without issues and that was when her love for writing really grew. She has always written in some form or fashion, starting out with poetry and song lyrics. She's always had a story in her head and voices talking to her. Thanks to lots of motivation from her husband, a wonderful laptop with a word processor, more hours than she could ever count, lots of sweat, blood, and tears, and blessings from the Lord God Almighty, she has finally managed to watch her dreams become a reality.

Stay Tuned For
Hollow of Treason
Book 2 in
The Euphoria Series
Coming Fall 2013